W9-AWA-617

Ellen Elizabeth Hunter

Ellen Eliz Hunter

Christmas Wedding

A Novella

Magnolia Mysteries

www.magnoliamysteries.com

Published by:
Magnolia Mysteries

This is a work of fiction.

ISBN 978-0-9755404-6-6

Cover and book design by Tim Doby

Also by Ellen Elizabeth Hunter

Murder on the Ghost Walk

Murder on the Candlelight Tour

Murder at the Azalea Festival

Murder at Wrightsville Beach

Murder on the ICW

Murder on the Cape Fear

Visit Ellen's website,
www.ellenhunter.com
Or contact her at:
ellenelizabethhunter@earthlink.net

ACKNOWLEDGEMENTS

A great big Thank You! to my wonderful readers. Without your interest, loyalty, and encouragement, where would I be? Where would Ashley and Melanie be? Certainly not marrying their loveable boyfriends and gearing up for future mysteries to solve.

In this book, Faye Brock has a cameo role, playing one of Melanie's gorgeous bridesmaids. In real life you'll find Faye at Century 21 Brock and Associates in Wilmington or at www.fayebrock.com.

And you can find Celebrity DJs, the talented DJ agency that had the guests dancing their feet off at the wedding reception, at www.celebrity-djs.com.

As always, I want to thank my talented designer Tim Doby for the beautiful cover.

1

"I declare, Melanie! You're becoming a regular bridezilla!" I accused my sister.

"I just want everything to be perfect for our wedding," she argued. "Don't you?"

"It will be perfect. I'm marrying darling Jon. You're marrying darling Cam — who is convinced you hung the moon, by the way. We've both kissed our requisite number of frogs, now we are marrying princes. So sure, it'll be perfect, even if we walk down the aisle wearing gunny sacks instead of Vera Wang dresses."

On a late Sunday afternoon, we were sitting outdoors at the Water Street Sidewalk Café, the weather as balmy as a fine Indian summer day. Overnight the Jet Stream had swept into Wilmington bearing warm breezes from the Caribbean. And even though we were experiencing another official Christmas season – the Candlelight Tour had been held two weekends ago, and the trees along the river were strung with fairy lights – it was warm enough to sit outside in the late afternoon with only a sweater draped over one's shoulders to ward off a practically non-existent chill. The Carolina coast is like that.

As usual we were discussing "the wedding," our double wedding that was set for Saturday, December 22, six days away. I am Ashley Wilkes, historic preservationist and old-house restorer. My sister Melanie is Wilmington's star realtor. She has been planning this most joyous event for almost a year.

Here on the restored riverfront, tourists mingled with locals. The unseasonably warm weather had brought day-trippers thronging to the coast and they were strolling Riverfront Park, or gazing up at the Alton Lennon Federal Building with its splashing water fountain, recalling how it had been the setting for Matlock's courthouse in the long-running, successful, and locally-filmed television series. At the dock, families with youngsters were lined up for the water taxi that would take them across the Cape Fear to the Battleship North Carolina.

Puffy little while clouds tracked across the blue sky and the river sparkled as brightly as the silver tinsel on the Christmas trees that adorned parlors throughout the historic district.

Directly across from the Water Street Restaurant's patio, the Henrietta III Riverboat tooted cheerfully, announcing that it was about to depart for a cruise down the Cape Fear.

Melanie who has inherited most of our family's fashion genes was dressed in the cinnamon-colored raw silk pantsuit that she had worn to church this morning. And as it was

Sunday I had eschewed my daily garb – what Melanie calls my construction wear chic — for a knit skirt and matching top in forest green. Every once in a while I like to show Melanie that my DNA includes fashion genes as well.

Melanie said, "I know our lives will be happy with the men we've chosen to marry. I'm not worried about that. I'm talking about the ceremony and the reception, and, oh, everything that's coming up. Everyone knows a zillion things can go wrong at the last minute. Oh, what will I do now that Colin has left and returned to New York?" she wailed. "How could he abandon me when I need him most?"

I covered her hand with my own. "Guess an invitation to decorate Hillary and Bill's Westchester home for their New Year's Eve party was too temping to resist."

"Guess so," she said woefully.

"Don't take it so hard, Mel. Colin Cowie completed our plans before he left. His signature is emblazoned on every aspect of this wedding. The cake design is magnificent."

Earlier we had been out to our caterer Elaine's bakery in Leland to check on the cakes with Celeste, a baker who is a wizard with cake floor and who creates flawless fondant. We had selected pear-vanilla cake with a cinnamon-cappuccino cream and hazelnut nougat filling — Celeste's own creation. She would begin baking the cake tomorrow, then assemble and decorate it during the week. There would be four square layers. Each layer would be spread with fondant that was skillfully sculpted to look like gift wrapping and ribbons on Christmas gift boxes. Life-like American Beauty red roses made from sugar would separate each layer and form a crown bouquet on top.

"The vendors have been selected and are ready to go," I reassured Melanie. "The big stuff is already contracted. And you've done a superb job. Everyone says so and I can't thank you enough for taking charge of our wedding. You can get along without Colin. You don't really need him anymore."

"Oh yes, I do," she said and paused to sip mineral water. She was determined not to gain an ounce – not that she ever does; not like me – and mineral water was the only beverage she was permitting herself these days. "Colin had such a soothing effect on my nerves. He kept me tranquil and calmed my jitters with that sweet, even temperament of his. And what exquisite taste!"

"Stop worrying, please Melanie. Aunt Ruby and I will step in to keep you calm."

The waitress arrived to take our orders. "Shouldn't we wait for the boys?" I asked.

"No, we'd better get our order in now. Cam had a meeting at the convention center. Then he and Jon were off on some mysterious mission together. All hush, hush, and whispering. I'm not sure when they'll be along, so let's go ahead and start without them."

I eyed a plate of the Southwestern Aztec Chicken being served at the next table. "Now, that's what I'd like to order." Witnessing her horrified expression, I quickly added, "But no, I won't order it."

"All that melted cheese! And the sour cream. You'd puff up like a balloon and never be able to squeeze into your wedding dress on Saturday," she exclaimed. Turning to the waitress, she said, "We'll share a Portabella Sandwich. And bring me another bottle of mineral water, please."

To me she said, "You having iced tea?"

"Of course," I replied.

"Unsweetened," she instructed the waitress.

"Half a mushroom sandwich, Melanie? Honestly! I know what I am going to do on my honeymoon."

She arched her eyebrows at me and grinned slyly. "Well, I should hope so."

"Not that," I said and laughed. "Well, that too, But first and foremost, I am going to eat! You have been starving me."

"You'll thank me later," she said smugly, her usual confident manner reasserting itself. "Now, you were speaking of Aunt Ruby. Let me tell you, Ashley, Aunt Ruby is acting mighty peculiar these days. I don't know what's gotten into her. Have you noticed?"

"No, I haven't seen her in days."

"That's just what I mean. And she wasn't at church this morning. And she and Binkie rarely miss church," she said.

"But I've been spending all of my time out at the waterway, Mel, finishing up the decorating of your house so you can move in after the honeymoon. Oh, and by the way, the trees are up and decorated and the draperies were hung in the master suite on Saturday. They look elegant. Now what's this about Aunt Ruby?"

"Well, she's just become so unavailable. She doesn't return my calls, and when she does, she makes excuses not to see me. She says she's busy. Busy doing what, I'd like to know. She's an old lady, what does she have to do, for pity sakes?"

"Maybe this big wedding is making her nervous," I offered.

Melanie shook her auburn hair vigorously. "I don't think so. Aunt Ruby has had a lifetime of experience at handling social events with aplomb. No, this is something else. I stopped by their house on Front Street after church, just to check on them, and she didn't come to the door. Her car was parked in that narrow driveway of theirs. Binkie's car wasn't there, but hers was."

"Well then. That's it. They went somewhere together in Binkie's car."

"No. I'm certain I saw a curtain twitch inside. She was there, just not answering the door or the phone. She's ignoring me, I tell you. And I just don't know why. Have I done something to offend her?"

"Mel, I don't believe that. Aunt Ruby and Binkie have been like parents to us since Mama and Daddy passed. Why wouldn't she want to see you? Especially at this special time. That doesn't make sense. She adores you. Just like we all do."

I knew the wedding plans had stressed Melanie out, but now her feverish brain was working overtime.

"She is supposed to be arranging for the soprano who is going to sing *Ave Maria* at the end of the prelude and right before the processional."

Melanie gave me a thoughtful look. "You don't think Aunt Ruby is sick, do you? Some dreadful disease? And she's not telling us because she doesn't want to spoil the wedding?"

"No, I don't think that. And I don't want you thinking that either. Here's our food," I announced brightly, but muttered to myself, "What little there is of it."

Two plates were set before us, a half sandwich on each

plate. I picked mine up and tried to munch on it slowly, tried not to scarf it down, but I was starving.

"Everything is going to be fine," I said for the umpteenth time between bites, trying to reassure her. "I have to say, it's a good thing my divorce was final in November. Otherwise, I'm sure you'd coerce me into committing bigamy just so the wedding could go off without a hitch!"

2

Melanie dropped her sandwich and cried, "Am I really that bad?"

"No," I said soothingly. "You've just been under a lot of stress, and you've got an overactive brain on the best of days. So try to relax. Thank goodness, Nick did not give me any trouble. He came through like a perfect gentleman. Went to the courthouse so I didn't have to. Signed all the papers. All I had to do was sign for the divorce decree when it was delivered to me."

"It's a wonder he wasn't traveling through Africa, or China. What a wanderer that man was," Melanie said, speaking of my former husband, Nicholas Yost, who when I met him had been a homicide detective with the Wilmington Police Department.

"By the way, the chief took him back. He's back on the force. Reinstated." I said.

"Oh, who gives a hoot? The man was a philanderer.

Dumping him was the smartest thing you ever did. And the bravest."

"He tried to explain that," I said, wondering why I was defending Nick. Perhaps it was simply that I didn't like being shown up for a fool. "He said that he was running away from deep feelings he was unprepared to face."

"Well, for pity sakes, who wants a man too weak to face his feelings? Cam is certainly not like that. And Jon isn't either."

"At least the divorce went smoothly." I continued. "We didn't fight over property. He didn't make a claim on my house and I didn't make a claim on the house he inherited from his father. And there are no babies to fight over," I added sadly.

Melanie swallowed the last of her half sandwich. "Look, baby sister, I know that having that miscarriage was hard for you. I know you won't get over it, and I won't make light of it. But a year has gone by, and surely it is a little easier for you now, isn't it?"

"Yes," I said. "It is easier. And having Jon to love and to love me has made me happier than I ever dreamed possible."

Melanie brightened. "Good. OK, now let's look at the paper again." She retrieved today's issue of *The New York Times* from the empty chair. She flipped *The Times* open to the wedding section.

"And here we are," she announced cheerfully. "Cam and I in *The New York Times* wedding section. I can't believe it. Do you know how hard it is to get in *The Times*? But my sweetie pie pulled some strings and we're in. And in color too.

Oh, I know, the four of us made the Wilmington paper and the Savannah paper, but *The New York Times*, well, that is celebrity status."

"I'm happy for you," I said, not caring about such things as much as she.

She stared at her picture critically. "I look OK, don't I?" she asked again.

"You look sensational, better than any New York deb," I assured her.

"Cam is considered one of the TV industry's most eligible bachelors, so that helped. And he knows important people. And I'm sure it helps that his mother is Nelda Cameron. I'm going to have this announcement framed."

"Not if you keep handling it," I said.

"Oh, this isn't the only copy I've got. There is a pristine copy in my car. And Cam bought a bundle. Now let's review the logistics one more time. Aunt Ruby and Binkie are going to pick up Kiki and Ray at the airport this evening."

She looked at her watch. "They should be leaving about now. Surely Aunt Ruby hasn't forgotten to do that."

"Melanie, stop worrying. Aunt Ruby is very reliable. And so is Binkie. If they say they are going to do something, they'll do it."

Aunt Ruby is our deceased mother's older sister, and Binkie is UNCW Professor Emeritus Benjamin Higgins, her husband of one year. They had been sweethearts as children and only rediscovered each other last year. They had never married until they found each other after a lifetime spent apart. Now they were happy to be spending their golden years as husband and wife.

"OK, then," Melanie said, checking off that item on the list she carried around in her wedding planner. "They will deliver Kiki and Ray to The Verandas where they have reservations. Aunt Ruby and Binkie will act as their hosts, showing them around town while we are busy with other pressing details. You haven't forgotten that we have a final fitting with the seamstress tomorrow. And then on Wednesday we will all go out to the airport to meet Nelda. She's flying in from Rome, you know."

"Oh, look," I called. "There are the boys now."

Jon and Cam were crossing the street toward us. Jon is tall, broad-shouldered and lean-waisted, with golden blonde hair and warm brown eyes. He has this little swagger when he walks, but just a little one that he is totally unaware of. He doesn't know how sexy he is, or how good looking. And I plan to keep it that way. But golly gee whiz wow, to quote my favorite movie character Holly Golightly, he sure makes my mouth water.

Melanie and I refer to them as "the boys" although they are certainly not "boys." Jon is thirty-four, the same age as Melanie. And Cameron Jordan, CEO of Gem Star Productions, recently celebrated his fortieth birthday. Melanie had pulled out all the stops on that birthday party. Melanie never does anything half-way. My sister is one high-energy lady.

"Hello, sweetheart," Cam said, dropping into the chair next to Melanie and brushing her lips with his own.

Jon gave me a hug and joined me, reaching for my hand

and giving it a little squeeze. His face lights up like a Christmas tree when he sees me, but his eyes said it all: I can't wait to get you alone.

"Ah, the wedding planner notebook is out and open and she's got her pen poised in her hand. She is going to work you to death, Ashley," Cam teased.

"You too," Melanie laughed and punched him lightly on the upper arm. "We've got your mother coming. I want everything to be special. Let me tell you what your jobs are for the week."

"Later, later," Cam laughed. "Right now, I need a nice cold beer."

"Me too," Jon said, and signaled a passing waiter.

While he placed their order, Melanie said to Cam, "What are you two up to? You both look like Cheshire cats. All smug and secretive."

"We'll never tell, will we, Jon?" Cam said jokingly.

Melanie glanced back down at her notes in the wedding planner. "How many brides get the famous Nelda Cameron at their weddings?" she asked.

"Only one that I know of," Cam said, teasingly.

Melanie gave him a soulful look. "I just want everything to go smoothly."

He hugged her. "Everything will be perfect. She'll take one look at you and fall madly in love with you the same way I did."

I studied the pair of them, and thought to myself, I sure hope he's right. But how often does a mother take one look at the woman her son is sleeping with and fall madly in love? Doesn't happen. The woman has got to prove herself first; prove that she is worthy.

3

"Now ain't this house grand!" Kiki exclaimed. "This place is palatial. Melanie done good for herself, kiddo."

On Monday, after our final bridal fittings, and trying on the lace jackets that we'd had designed and sewn to cover our arms when we were outside, I picked up Kiki at The Verandas and brought her out to Melanie's newly restored lodge to show it off.

"Say, Ashley, do you remember that one-bedroom apartment on lower Fifth Avenue that we shared with two other girls back in our Parsons' days?"

Kiki and I had been roommates when we were students at Parsons School of Design in New York City.

"How could I ever forget? A pull-out sofa in the living room for the other two girls. You and I were lucky enough to share the tiny bedroom, two twin beds pushed against the walls and still there was barely space to walk between them. I remember keeping my clothes in my trunk at the foot of the bed because there simply wasn't closet space. And forget about a dresser."

Kiki was trembling with laughter. "I remember that well. We used to kid you and ask you when you were hopping on the train."

"Still, I wouldn't trade that experience for anything," I mused aloud. After earning my MFA at Parsons, I'd returned south to get a Master's degree in Historic Preservation from the Savannah College of Art and Design. Then I'd come home for good, to take up my profession of old-house restoration.

"Come on," I said to Kiki, "let me show you around inside." We strolled on flagstones through the great arched entrance into a reception hall that extended past a broad oak staircase and led back to the waterway side of the house.

"Here's the lowdown on this house, Kiki. It's an old hunting lodge that was built during the Gilded Age when gentlemen acquired hunting preserves and constructed lodges as retreats for themselves and their buddies. Then they'd get drunk as skunks and shoot at anything that moved."

Leading her into the drawing room, I pointed to the upper portion of immensely high walls. "There were buck heads mounted up there. I took a great deal of pleasure in removing them. A barbaric tradition."

We strolled to the center of the huge drawing room. "Melanie bought this house from a friend of hers from their pageant days, Crystal Lynne, recently widowed. She's one of the bridesmaids. You'll get to meet her at the bridesmaid's dinner."

"Wednesday night, right? I'll be there with bells on."

"Yes, Wednesday. How are you getting along with Aunt Ruby? She's looking after you and Ray, isn't she?" I asked, mindful of Melanie's suspicions that Aunt Ruby was not behaving like herself.

"She's a grand lady, that aunt of yours. She and Ray were driving the singer to the church so she could practice *Ave Maria* with the pianist there. You remember how Ray loves the opera."

"Oh, good," I said, relieved that the plans were proceeding on schedule.

"Kiki, you should have seen this place. Falling apart. Holes in the roof that let in rain. Anybody with a truck and a screw driver would drive up that lane, and raid the place of irreplaceable valuables. It has taken Jon and me and our general contractor Willie Hudson and his crew almost a year to bring things back to close to their original state. Better, actually, because we don't use dead animals as decorative accessories."

"You did a splendid job, gal friend, and I'm proud of you. The style reminds me of the Biltmore House," Kiki said.

"It's supposed to. Melanie and I made countless trips to Asheville to tour Biltmore and get ideas. You aren't allowed to photograph the interiors, but every time the guard looked the other way, Melanie would sneak in a shot. When she got caught, she'd just give him that megawatt smile of hers and say sweetly, 'I'm so sorry, officer, I won't do it again.' And she didn't. Not until his back was turned." I laughed, remembering my sister's audacity.

"I just love that sister of yours," Kiki said. "She knows that charm will get you pretty much anything you want out of people."

Kiki's sense of admiration was not returned by Melanie. Melanie thought Kiki was "strange" and if truth be told, Melanie was rather intimidated by Kiki. Melanie is not intimidated easily. But indeed, Kiki was no ordinary woman. She was larger than life, actually. A really big woman, not fat, just big. Big bones and plenty of muscle on those bones. Huge, animated black eyes that crackled with life and joy. A large full mouth that was always laughing. And the outlandish way she dressed! Bold patterns and colors. But they suited her. There was no missing Kiki. She stood out in any crowd, and had gone on to become a successful celebrity decorator.

Melanie felt overwhelmed by her. But Kiki persisted in loving Melanie.

"Are you waiting until after the wedding to furnish this room?" she asked. "Those marble fireplaces are totally impressive. And just look at those Christmas trees, they must be twelve feet high."

"We're going to hold the reception here," I said. "And we're making the most of the Christmas theme." Three beautifully decorated trees filled three of the corners.

"The herringbone parquet floor will be perfect for dancing. The DJ will set up over in that fourth corner. Our deal with an orchestra fell through. But Melanie found a super DJ service out of Raleigh called Celebrity DJs. Very experienced, very professional."

"Sounds cool," Kiki said, strolling around the huge room and taking it all in.

"Yes, they helped us select the music, then they arrange it all so that one song segues into the next. Blending, I think it's called. And the DJ acts as the Master of Ceremonies as well.

"But to answer your question about the furnishings, we've purchased just about everything for this room. It's all in storage until after the honeymoon. And Kiki, we shopped locally. There's a nice little antique district on Castle Street. I'll take you out there if time permits. If not, you can walk over from The Verandas. And we found gems at The Ivy Cottage, a huge consignment shop.

"For the reception, Colin designed round tables for this room. There will be fifteen tables that seat ten each, so one hundred and fifty guests. Melanie wanted to invite everyone in town and set up tents on the lawn. But Colin persuaded her to winnow the guest list to one hundred and fifty so that a place on it would be coveted."

"Clever! Now you know why he is so in demand," Kiki chimed in.

I went on, "The head table will be over there. Our color scheme is red, white and gold. The tables will have floor-length white brocade cloths. The chairs are gold and they will have garlands of red roses draped across the backs. The entire reception décor is 'so Colin.'"

"He's the best," Kiki agreed.

"The centerpieces will be red rose bouquets atop little trees. The china will be red with gold. Gold vermeil flatware. And gold rims on the glassware."

"Sounds divine!"

"It will be. But we almost had a catastrophe. Melanie and I were watching *Platinum Weddings* on TLC. They featured a half million dollar wedding. Well, soon Melanie began berating herself because she had not selected jeweled table cloths and a twelve-piece orchestra plus a string quartet."

"Those weddings are over the top," Kiki said. "Absolutely grotesque."

"That is exactly what I told her. I said, 'Melanie, those kind of weddings run counter to everything Colin stands for. You were so thrilled to get him to design the wedding. Colin is known for his understated elegance, for weddings and parties where people are the focal point, not some rhinestone embossed table cloth."

"So what happened?" Kiki asked.

"Well, she wasn't convinced. So I said to her, 'Melanie, are you aware that fifty percent of the world's population lives on two dollars a day? Given that, doesn't a half-million dollar wedding sound like the height of insensitivity?

"She saw the light then. Still, this is all really more than Jon and I ever wanted. This is Melanie's dream. Did you see the Sunday *Times* yesterday? Melanie and Cam made the Wedding page. Melanie is beside herself with excitement."

"Well, hey, don't knock it. Most brides would kill to get their picture in the Sunday *Times*," Kiki said.

"OK, you and Melanie have convinced me. I am not *Lifestyle* material. Now come on, I'll show you the rest of the downstairs."

"Ashley, I appreciate it that you permitted us bridesmaids to select our own dresses. The dress I chose suits me fine," she said as we moved back into the reception hall. "None of that frou frou little girl stuff for me."

We have given each bridesmaid a swatch of the color they were to wear – a bright Christmassy red – but let them choose the style that suited their figure type. Subject to Melanie's approval, of course. She had to have the last word.

"Remember those big tulle dresses your mother made you wear to her mock wedding to my grandfather?" Kiki reminisced.

"How could I forget? Melanie's was green and she said she looked like Kermit the frog. But then the wedding was cancelled because of that poor lady's sudden death."

"And they never rescheduled. Granddad was heart broken."

"Oh, poor man. But you mean Rhett, don't you?" I asked, referring to the name Mama had given to Kiki's grandfather when she met him at the Magnolia Manor Nursing Home. Mama had been besotted with *Gone With the Wind*.

"He loved it that she called him Rhett. Made him feel young and dashing, he said, like Clark Gable. He adored your mother," Kiki said with a wistful smile. "He died about six months after she did."

I gave her a hug but my arm didn't quite make it around her formidable girth. "I know you miss him, Kiki."

4

Kiki brushed away a tear. "What's back here?" she asked with false bravado.

"This is the garden room. We modeled it after the one at Biltmore, but on a smaller scale. It's octagonal, like theirs, but the waterway side is all glass."

And the domed roof was made of glass too, supported by I-beam steel trusses that were then covered with oak, just as the garden room roof at the Biltmore House had been constructed.

The garden room extended out from the rear of the lodge, and through the windows there were breathtaking views of the Intracoastal Waterway, and beyond that, of Wrightsville Beach. A sleek white yacht went sailing past, bound for the Wrightsville Marina.

The waterway doesn't change much in appearance from season to season. The live oak trees are always green, as are the magnolia trees. The sky and the water look summer-time blue even in January. And with the golden sea grasses and the colorful cottages, it could be June, not December.

"This room is lovely, Ashley. I love the palm trees, and all those orchids. And look at this beautiful antique rattan furniture. Oh, and the three-tiered water fountain. And that darling cupid on top. Does it work?"

"Oh, it works. We'll have it flowing during the reception."

"You know, Ashley, I just might borrow this concept for the house I'm decorating for the mayor of Charlotte on Queen's Road. Would you mind?"

Kiki's trip to North Carolina was half-work, half-play. She'd be driving back and forth to her decorating job in Charlotte. Ray was here to play, she'd said, and he had already chartered a yacht and planned a cruise.

"Mind?" I asked. "Why would I mind? Didn't I borrow the idea from Richard Morris Hunt?"

"Fair's fair," she said.

"We're going to hold the Kindness Ceremony out here during the reception," I said.

"What's a Kindness Ceremony?" Kiki asked.

"Something Melanie dreamed up. You'll see. You'll like it."

Kiki rolled her big beautiful eyes. "Like I always said: That sister of yours is not just another pretty face. You know, Ray has been carrying the torch for her for the past two years. He tried dating, but he couldn't get Melanie out of his heart. He is totally crushed that she is marrying someone else."

Oh no, I thought to myself.

Kiki went on, "Just between you and me, I think he intends to bare his soul and ask her if she's sure she wants to go through with her marriage to Cam. He's just waiting for the right time to get her alone."

"Please don't say that. We're all as twitchy as cats on a porch full of rocking chairs. Are you sure?"

Kiki rolled her eyes again. "That's what he confided on the plane ride down. Maybe he'll see her with Cam and decide it's hopeless for him. Maybe this is what he needs to get unstuck. I sure know why they call it being 'stuck' on someone. You can't move forward, you can't move back. You are totally stuck. But he's my brother and I love him so I hate to see him hurting."

"Of course you do," I agreed. "But, Kiki, Ray's no ordinary man. He's rich and successful and so handsome. He could have anyone."

"He don't want anyone, kiddo. He wants what he can't have," Kiki said, her love for her brother shinning through. "Ain't that always the way?"

Then she said, "Let's change the subject. I'm looking forward to all the festivities. Who knows? I may take the plunge myself one day."

"Oh, is there someone special?" I asked, and hoped there was. Kiki was a great girl.

"Not right now, but you never know. Love is just around the corner. Or staring you right in the face. You're living proof of that, aren't you?"

"I am," I said, and felt myself smile broadly.

"Uhmmm, Kiki . . . before I drive you back to town, I was wondering . . ."

"Spit it out, girl! You can say anything to me. You oughta know that by now."

"Well, do you have your cards with you, by any chance?"

Kiki reared back and let out a roar of laughter. "Have you ever known me to be without my cards? 'Course I got my cards. In my bag. You need a reading?"

"I do, Kiki. There is something strange going on. Aunt Ruby is acting peculiar; she's unavailable which is so unlike her. Melanie is as jumpy as a grasshopper. Cam's mother, the incomparable Nelda Cameron, is arriving on Wednesday."

"I know Nelda. That's right, she is Cam's mother."

"You know Nelda?"

"Yep. Decorated her Park Avenue apartment. Only why she wanted it redecorated beats me. The lady lives ten months out of the year in Rome."

"Well, Melanie is a wreck worrying about meeting her," I said.

"Melanie hasn't met her yet?"

"No," I answered, "somehow that never happened. All pretty strange to me. Jon drove me to Lumberton and insisted I meet Granny Campbell just as soon as we became engaged. She is all he has."

"Oh wow, Melanie hasn't met Nelda, huh?" For an instant she looked worried. "Well, hey, Nelda is all right. You've just got to know how to handle her. You know, she has spent her whole life with people kowtowing to her, so she thinks she can walk all over everyone. You've just got to stand up to her, that's all. That way she'll respect you."

"I'll be sure to tell Melanie," I said.

"OK, babe, let me get my bag. We'll sit out here among these gorgeous orchids and I'll do a reading for you and see if we can't put your mind at ease."

"Thanks," I said, relieved. Kiki was the mistress of the Tarot cards. And as she was fond of saying: The cards never lie.

"OK, you remember how we do this?" she asked after she had returned from the car with her tote bag.

"I draw the cards," I responded.

"You draw ten cards from the seventy-eight. Those ten cards will represent your journey at this particular moment. The immediate situation, as well as its probable outcome, will be revealed."

Kiki unwrapped the deck from its traditional black cloth wrapping. She spread out the cloth, shuffled the cards, then laid them face down on the table in a fan shape. "So OK now Ashley, draw ten cards."

I selected ten cards at random, then handed them in order to Kiki who spread them in the Celtic Cross pattern on the black cloth.

Turning over the first card, Kiki said, "This first card is called the Significator. This card reflects your current situation. Aha! Now you know why I say the cards never lie. Here we have The Empress. Look at her, a beautiful earthy woman, and very pregnant."

"Oh, Kiki, you know how much I want children."

"Let's not go jumping the gun here, kiddo. The Empress represents the Great Mother, the maternal instinct. Her appearance in the cards means that you are beginning an earthier phase of life. She portends marriage. How appropriate with your wedding just days away. Now, let's see what is crossing the Significator, that which will be generating conflict and obstructing your destiny."

"Maybe it will be a blank card," I joked.

Kiki turned over the crossing card and we both peered at the picture of yet another woman seated on a golden throne, the arms of which were engraved with golden snakes. In one hand she held a golden apple; in the other she held a golden cup.

"The Queen of Cups," Kiki said. "Helen of Troy. Wife of King Menelaus, whose love affair with Paris was the excuse for starting the Trojan War. I personally think she got a bum rap. Men are always blaming women when their testosterone-induced misadventures fail to pan out."

"But what does this mean? A war? Feuding in my family? Or between Jon and me? Please say no."

Kiki looked me straight in the eye. "Well, you will have to tell me who she is."

"But I don't know. Someone representing a feud?" I shrugged my shoulders. "I simply don't know. We've all been getting along rather well, considering the pressure we are under."

Kiki offered, "Melanie is a beauty, just like Helen. But there's no getting around it, the Queen of Cups signifies the coming of crisis and conflict. Maybe you'd better find out who this mysterious woman is before it is too late."

"I will. I'll be on the look-out for her."

"Good for you."

One by one Kiki flipped the cards, each suggesting that the wedding would not go smoothly. When we came to the tenth card, I held my breath, for it is called the Final Outcome, the predictor of what is to come.

"The Chariot!" we shouted together at the image of a warrior driving a chariot, pulled by two sturdy horses.

"Here we have aggression, conflict, stubborn wills, and a struggle which you must overcome."

Kiki gave me a shrewd look. "Honey, whatever is coming, you've got a fight on your hands. But it'll be worth it. You can't argue with the cards. And their message is loud and clear: you can't run from this fight, you're gonna have to slug it out."

5

"I swear, Jon, I would not believe it if I hadn't seen her with my own eyes. Melanie is having a fling with Kiki's brother, Ray. And the wedding is only three days away!" I moaned, and dropped my face into my palms.

Jon, my sweetie and husband-to-be, reached over from the driver's side and patted my knee. "Take a deep breath, Ashley, and then slowly tell me exactly what you saw. When and where. Don't leave anything out."

I lowered my hands to my lap and lifted my gaze to my wonderful fiancé. He had been my respected business partner first, then my trusted best friend, now he is my lover. Jon Campbell, architect, romantic guy and incredible lover.

And he is mine. All mine. Lucky me. Jon and I had met for the second time three years ago when we worked together on our first house restoration. The first time we had met I had been fourteen and he had been twenty-two and studying architecture at NC State.

"Melanie has been consumed with planning this lavish double wedding for the past year, and now she's about to ruin everything and risk her chance at happiness with Cam by getting involved with Ray," I complained to Jon.

Ray is known as "The Wizard of Wall Street", the youngest futures trader on the street with his very own seat on the New York Stock Exchange. I remember when he'd met Melanie two years ago and how smitten he'd been with her. And as I remember, she'd been pretty gaga over him too. He'd invited us both to New York to be his guests, and we did go, but by then Melanie, true to form, had gotten involved with someone else. She'd always been romantically involved with someone, usually a sleazy guy who was unworthy of her. Isn't that the way it goes? You have a woman who is a winner attracted to men who are losers.

I glanced out of the window of Jon's Escalade at Smith's Creek and the swampy landscape that flew by as we drove out to the airport. We were meeting Melanie and Cam there, all of us come to fetch Cam's famous mother and whisk her off to The Verandas Bed and Breakfast where the spoiler Ray was bedding down as well. But was he bedding down with my sister? That was the question on my mind.

"You know, she always used that 'grass is greener' expression. Then she'd go off with the most dangerous man in the crowd. At least Ray is not dangerous. He's a sweetheart, actually. But poor Cam. He's the best thing that ever happened to her. If she messes this up, I'll disown her," I vowed to Jon.

"You still haven't told me what you saw that has got you so upset." He turned briefly to give me a heart-stopping smile.

Jon has mastered the art of remaining calm and cool when I get worked up into a tizzy.

"I was sitting out on the porch, waiting for you to drive up. I happened to notice a red convertible pull in at The Verandas."

I live in a restored Queen Anne style house on Nun Street, across the street and a few doors east of the popular bed and breakfast.

"The top was down. Can you believe this weather? Almost Christmas and people are driving around in open convertibles! Must be global warming."

"Ashley, calm down. You're babbling."

"I am, aren't I? Sorry. Anyway, Melanie was driving. Ray was on the passenger side. And before he got out, they kissed. And I don't mean a friendly little peck on the check. Or even a brief kiss on the lips. I mean a long, lingering, makes you weak in the knees, soulful K-I-S-S."

"Oh, no. I've seen your sister pull some crazy stunts, but this is so selfish and thoughtless. Has she said anything to you? Are she and Cam having second thoughts?"

He answered his own question. "No, he wouldn't be. As far as Cameron Jordan is concerned, there is only one woman on this earth, and that is Melanie. I agree with you. He is the best thing that has ever happened to her. He's a great guy and I count him as my best friend.

"So, has Melanie hinted that she is getting cold feet?"

"Not a peep. But then all we ever talk about these days are the wedding plans. As if the reason we are having this wedding has gotten lost in the quest for perfect roses, perfect menus, perfect music. You know. And to tell you the truth, Jon, she has been hard to reach since Sunday, which is coincidentally when Ray arrived. She never picks up when I call her on her cell. And often she fails to return my calls. Claims she is too busy with the wedding.

"And she is doing the same thing to Cam. He called me this morning looking for her. She was not answering her cell when he called to verify that she was meeting us at the airport."

"You think she was with Ray?" Jon asked.

"I'm worried that she was with him all night, and that when I saw her she was returning him to the B&B."

Jon shook his head. "I just wanted us to have a simple, sweet wedding surrounded by the people we love. We don't need these theatrics in our life."

"I'm with you. But to answer your question, no, I don't think she is going to cancel the wedding because Ray has turned up in her life again. But it seems to me that she is hell bent on having herself one last torrid fling before she settles down."

Jon exited onto Airport Boulevard. "I sure hope she does not break a few hearts in the process. Including her own."

We arrived at ILM in plenty of time and found Melanie and Cameron waiting for us in the Tailwind Bar just outside of Security Screening. They were having iced tea and Jon and I ordered tall frosty glasses as well. It wouldn't do for us to meet Melanie's new mother-in-law with alcohol on our breaths.

Melanie must have driven straight here after dropping Ray off at The Verandas. She is the world's speediest driver who could teach Kyle Petty a thing or two. She knows every traffic cop in New Hanover County on a first name basis, but because she has sold many of them their homes, they usually let her off with a grim warning about the consequences of a crash at a high speed.

"Most of the guests are arriving today and tomorrow," I said brightly, telling Melanie and Cam what they already knew. "But Kiki and Ray flew in from New York on Sunday and are all settled at The Verandas. You remember Kiki and Ray, don't you, Melanie?" I knew just how well Melanie remembered Ray, I just wanted to see her reaction to the mention of his name.

As usual my older sister looked stunning in an olive green and cream sweater set and flirty skirt with high heeled pumps. Her long auburn hair was loose and wavy. I had on straight-legged jeans and loose-knit white sweater.

You could see how much Cam adored Melanie by the admiring glances he cast her way. For an internationally successful television and motion picture producer, Cam was an unassuming, sweet kind of guy who wore his heart on his sleeve. I don't know if he was inexperienced with women or if it was simply that Melanie had knocked him off his feet.

He had on a navy suit and a green and blue tie, and although his clothes were nicely tailored and obviously expensive, Cam always had this rumpled quality about his attire, plus it seemed impossible for him to keep his tousled hair neat.

Melanie reached out to smooth down his hair in a motherly sort of way before she replied sharply to my question. "Kiki and Ray? Of course I remember them. Who could forget that weird woman, with her outlandish flowing garments, and that gruff voice? You'd never think that they were brother and sister. Ray is polished, and handsome, a real go-getter."

"Then you haven't seen them yet?" I asked sweetly.

"Sorry. Can't say I've had that pleasure," she replied with her mouth set in a grim expression.

So that was how she was going to play it. Melanie was admitting to nothing. Yet less than an hour ago I had seen her kissing Ray passionately outside The Verandas. Now here she was sitting innocently, holding hands with her fiancé.

Oh, Daddy, why aren't you here when I need you? Well, somebody had to save her from ruining her life. And as usual I guess that person would have to be me. With Jon's help.

6

Nelda Cameron had been known as America's sweetheart back in the fifties. Star of stage and screen, she had won an academy award in 1956 for her starring role in a suspense thriller directed by Cam's father, Harvey Jordan. After his death, she had never remarried.

Although, according to Melanie who got it from Cam, she had not lacked for male companionship. She was just too savvy to marry one of her younger leading men, and thus saved Cam from the consequences and the embarrassment of having a step-father his own age.

That Cam had turned out to be such a nice guy was nothing short of a minor miracle, according to Melanie.

At age seventy, Nelda still had the looks and presence to make heads turn. She swept through the concourse dressed in one of her long, flowing signature outfits. She was still featured as a fashion icon in ladies' magazines. But with a figure not quite as willowy as in her youth, she had adopted silky pastel outfits with flowing fingertip jackets, silky wide-leg trousers, and attractively draped scarves.

"Cameron!" she called in her rich contralto voice as she hurried to throw her arms around her son so fiercely it was if they had been separated at his birth. It was a touching scene. They embraced and it was clear to us as we stood apart and watched that Cameron was delighted to be reunited with his mother.

After hugging and kissing, they stepped back to hold each other at arms length and gazed adoringly at each other. "I swear, Mother, you never age. You have discovered the fountain of youth."

"Only the Trevi fountain," Nelda declared with a rich, deep laugh.

To me she came across in real life exactly as she did on the Turner Movie Classics channel. Her hair was still golden blonde, her eyes still pale blue with attractive laugh lines at the outer corners. She still looked like America's sweetheart. So was she acting? Or was there no difference between her silver screen persona and her real life persona as Cam's mother?

Then she reached up and brushed back Cam's unruly lock of tousled light brown hair, exactly as I had seen Melanie do only minutes earlier. Uh oh. That gesture was a sign of ownership, a public display of "I can touch him but you cannot" privilege.

For a fraction of a second her gaze turned brittle as she sized up the rest of us. Her eyes swept over Jon, then me, then alighted on Melanie. The look she gave Melanie was critically appraising, but for only a half-second. Then her academy award-winning training reasserted itself, and she smiled and exclaimed, "And you must be Melanie. I'd know you anywhere, my dear. Cam has described you perfectly." She seized Melanie's hands in her own and stood gazing benevolently at her.

Jon and I exchanged guarded glances. Nelda and Melanie had never met. On their trips to New York, Cam had suggested they all get together but Nelda had always had some reason why they could not meet. A prior commitment, a little virus she'd picked up on the plane flight from Rome, a sudden but important trip to Los Angeles. Thus, Melanie had never met her future mother-in-law. Until this moment – three days before the wedding.

Cam introduced Jon and me and she greeted us charmingly. Everything about Nelda Cameron was charming. Everything was sweet and light. But I did not fall for her act for one moment. This was a woman with nerves of steel, with determination and drive, who knew exactly what she wanted and how to get it.

For once, Melanie was outmatched.

That became even more obvious as our party moved through the concourse toward the baggage claim area. Although Nelda's tone was sweet and undemanding, without a trace of rancor, still the gist of what she told Cam was out-and-out criticism. "Cam, darling, I simply don't understand why you and Melanie could not come to Rome to be married. Why are you getting married in this quaint little town, which is perfectly darling I am sure, but still we are among strangers, and I don't know a soul?"

Before Cam could reply, she went on, "Now darling, your old mother still has a bit of influence, and a word or two in the right ears and you and your wedding party will be staying at the Hotel Hassler – that's where Tom Cruise and Katie Holmes stay when they are in Rome – and the wedding ceremony will be held in one of Rome's oldest and most elegant palazzos. All of Roman society will attend, and you'll get international media coverage. Instead, you, the son of Hollywood giants, are marrying in a little town no one has ever heard of."

Nelda had linked arms with Cam and the two of them walked ahead but her words carried to the three of us who trailed along behind like peasants following a royal procession.

"Oh, I'm sure it is all quite lovely here," she continued, "but not at all on our social level and not what your father and I raised you to choose."

Melanie's face was growing red with suppressed fury.

Nelda stopped and faced Cam squarely. "It's not too late, darling. One word from me and there are people in Rome just waiting to spring into action. We could have the wedding on New Year's Day."

She smiled brightly as if he would jump at the chance to cancel his wedding here and fly off to Rome with or without Melanie. And wasn't Melanie precisely at the heart of her criticism? Any fool could see the problem for Nelda was not the town. The problem was that her darling little boy had grown up and was getting married. No woman would be good enough.

Cam's eyebrows scrunched together into a straight line and his face grew dark.

Jon gave me a mystified look. What is wrong with her, he seemed be asking.

"You wait here, mother," Cam said after we had stacked her luggage on the sidewalk. "I'll just get the car."

"Hurry, dear," she said. "I can't wait to see your house."

She turned to us, "My son has been living here in South Carolina for almost two years and he has never invited his mother to see his home."

"This is North Carolina," Jon said evenly.

Nelda reached into her handbag and withdrew large dark sunglasses. "My, it is bright here," she said. Then added airily, "North Carolina? South Carolina? What difference does it make?"

Cam said, "Mother, I <u>have</u> invited you to visit my home. Many times. But you wouldn't come. Don't say I didn't ask you here."

"Oh, well, I'm in my dotage, son. Don't pay any attention to what I say. I do get things mixed up. I'm not so young anymore, remember?"

"Oh, mother," Cam said with a groan.

Out of Nelda's view, Melanie rolled her eyes heavenward. Then she too donned huge sunglasses and said, "My car is off in the other direction. And I have an appointment." For a moment the corners of her mouth lifted. She was pleased about something. Either her appointment or being rid of, if only temporarily, Cam's mother. "Ashley, I'll see you later at the bridesmaids' dinner."

"Mother," Cam said, "you are not staying at my house. It's way out of town and inconvenient. Besides, I'm in the midst of packing so you wouldn't be comfortable there."

"Oh, are you moving, dear?" Nelda asked absently.

"Yes, mother. Of course, I'm moving. Melanie and I bought a hunting lodge together. Ashley and Jon have restored it for us, and we'll be settling in after the honeymoon. I've told you all this."

Nelda lifted a finger to her lips. "Yes, I had forgotten."

"So Mother, we are putting you up at the The Verandas, which is right downtown and close to the church and to the Bellamy Mansion where we're holding the rehearsal dinner."

"And I'm not staying at your house with you?" Nelda asked in a pathetic little voice.

"Well, uhmmm, I didn't realize it would matter to you," Cam said apologetically.

You could see he was torn.

"Well, I'll just be off," Melanie said eagerly. "It was so lovely meeting you, Mrs. Cameron."

"Call me Nelda," Nelda said absently. "No, wait, Melanie. You get your car and bring it around. I'll drive into town with you. And you come too, Ashley."

She smiled confidently. "That way we can get to know each other. Just we three girls, as it were. Won't that be cozy?"

Melanie concealed her true feelings well. She gave Nelda one of her dazzling smiles, the kind she had learned to perfect for the judges during her pageant days. "Oh, yes, cozy. Yes, let us girls drive into town together. I wouldn't miss this chance for us to get to know each other better."

Her voice dripped honey. Now that Melanie had Nelda's number, perhaps she was going to be a match for her future mother-in-law after all.

"There, Nelda, that is St. James," Melanie said, driving slowly past the stately Gothic Revival church. "That is where we'll be married on Saturday. The Wilkes family have been members here for four generations."

I leaned forward from the back seat and said to Nelda, "The parish was founded in 1729."

"Hardly old when compared to the churches in Italy," Nelda said with a sniff of her nose.

"I know, Nelda. I have toured Italy. So has Melanie. We love Italy's old churches. But we are also proud of our own."

"Why, of course you are, dear." She made a show of looking over both sides of Market Street. "This is a dear little town."

We continued east on Market, circling around the Kenan Memorial Fountain. Melanie pointed to the immense dazzlingly white mansion. "That is the Bellamy Mansion," she told Nelda. "We're holding the rehearsal dinner there on Friday night. It's within walking distance of the church."

Again, I leaned forward. "Melanie's friend Elaine is catering the rehearsal dinner and the reception. Elaine is the best."

"We've been friends since high school," Melanie said.

"How precious," Nelda commented.

Driving west again, Melanie drove past the Burgwin-Wright House and explained how it had been the headquarters of Lord Cornwallis during the Revolutionary War. Nelda had no comment to that.

"That is the oldest standing building in the town," I said, pointing to the Mitchell-Smith-Anderson House. "It was built in 1740."

Still no comment from our guest.

"Since I cancelled my appointment so we could have this little tour," Melanie said with a sweetness so syrupy any one should know it was fake, "we have time to show you the restored riverfront."

Nelda sniffed. "No. Don't bother. Just take me to the hotel."

"Oh, we'll be delighted to deliver you any place you say," Melanie said without a trace of sarcasm in her tone.

"We ought to dump her in the river," I muttered under my breath.

7

Our nice weather was holding and according to the weather man would continue throughout the weekend. Then, in time for Christmas, we'd get a cold front next week. When our local weather man talks about a cold front, he is referring to temperatures in the fifties and sixties, rarely freezing.

A few hours after dropping Nelda Cameron at The Verandas, I changed into slacks and a sweater and drove out to Airlie Road to meet the bridesmaids at the Bridge Tender restaurant for dinner. Melanie had told us to dress casually, and we'd all turned up in slacks and jeans, with sweaters and hoodies. Since the evening was pleasant we opted for a large table on the deck.

"Ain't this weather grand?" Kiki asked everyone in her hearty, booming voice. She introduced herself to the other girls. She'd been in Charlotte, working on her decorating project for the mayor yesterday and today. "I'll be driving back to Charlotte after this dinner," she told me. "But I'll be here for the rehearsal and the rehearsal dinner on Friday. I like driving. And I don't get much chance to drive in New York."

"I miss driving too," Kelly Lauder said. "I live in New York also," she told Kiki, Candy Murray, and Faye Brock, whom she'd never met.

Kelly and Crystal Lynne had grown up in Wilmington, and Faye in Southport. "We're used to having June in December," Crystal Lynne said.

"And we all know who you are, Kelly," Faye said with a dazzling smile. "I can't walk into CVS without seeing your pretty face on the cover of a magazine."

And then everyone was talking at once, explaining about their careers, their families. Faye was married to Danny Brock, the president of the North Carolina Association of Realtors, and they were both good friends of Melanie's. And Candy was married to Bo Murray who ran a Cadillac dealership in Greensboro. The others girls were single. Crystal Lynne was a widow. I was the only divorcee in the group. I detest failure. But not this time, I promised myself. This time I've got a winner.

We decided white wine would do us the least harm and ordered two bottles for the table. As the waiter did the honors, I glanced at Melanie and gave her a wink. This was fun. Very festive. We were in our element. Letting our hair down – just the girls.

But there was one fly in my white wine and I remembered him. "Kiki, what has Ray been doing this week?"

"He chartered a yacht yesterday and spent the day and the night out on the water." She looked out over the waterway to the spanking white yachts tied up at the Wrightsville Marina across Motts Channel. "I gotta get me one of those some day."

The talk turned to boating and water sports.

"Oh, and speaking of yachts, wait until you hear this," Melanie said loudly. "The boys, as you know, are holding their bachelor party on Cam's yacht. And you'll never guess who invited herself. My future mother-in-law, Nelda Cameron! Nelda crashed the bachelor's party."

The bridesmaids laughed. They had been hearing stories about Nelda's snooty behavior and the way she looked down on the town we all loved. She was not scoring any Brownie points with these girls, despite her famous reputation.

Across the channel Blue Water Restaurant was doing a brisk outdoor business in the pleasantly warm evening. And there were people on the pedestrian walkway of the drawbridge just off to our right.

I glanced at Melanie. Had she spent the night with Ray on the yacht? And had they been returning from a night together when I saw her kissing him in front of The Verandas that morning? I hadn't a clue.

"Now we don't want to overeat," Melanie said, "so we can fit into our dresses. I'd recommend the Asian Tuna, very tasty, and not fattening."

"Naturally you'd think of that, gal friend," Kiki told Melanie with a bellowing laugh. "All you itty bitty girls can eat raw tuna if you want. I'm a meat and potatoes girl, myself. I'm going for the steak. I never gain weight. I got big at sixteen and I've stayed the same size ever since."

Everyone smiled, but no one asked her what size that was. Even I didn't know.

"We have a little something for all of you," I said, and dipped my hand into the shopping bag at my feet. I handed out presents, and there were shrills of delight as the gift boxes were opened to reveal shiny gold quilted wallets.

"I love mine," someone said.

"Oh, I need a new wallet," another said.

Melanie stood, raising her wine glass high in the air. "I'd like to make a toast to all you girls whom I love so much. To Crystal Lynne, and Candy, and . . ."

Melanie's wine glass exploded in her hand. One moment she was holding a glass of white wine. The next moment, the glass flew apart, raining glass shards and white wine on the table.

Everyone screamed, including diners at other tables. Then we jumped up and scattered, away from the glass littered table.

Melanie was speechless, still holding the stem of the glass in her hand, and wearing the most astonished expression.

"I've never seen anything like it!" someone shouted.

Two waiters appeared, saw the disaster, and ran for the manager. He arrived quickly. "Cover that mess with a table cloth," he instructed. "We'll clean up later."

Turning to us, he said, "Ladies, I am so sorry. We've never experienced such an accident. We pride ourselves on safety. Please, don't be alarmed. We'll move you to another table. Order whatever you want. This dinner is on me."

The girls were positively twittering. "I don't believe it," Candy said. "That glass exploded all by itself."

Everyone was talking at once, speculating. Melanie's face had grown white.

Everyone was talking but Kiki, who looked dark, solemn, and pensive.

8

I was meeting Melanie for lunch at Aunt Ruby's on Thursday. But on Thursday morning I had, unbelievably, nothing on my calendar so I spent the morning lolling in bed with my honey. I described the breaking glass incident.

"The glass must have had a crack," he guessed. "So that when the waiter poured the cold wine into it, it shattered."

"It exploded, Jon. I've never seen anything like it."

"Was anyone hurt?" he asked.

"No. Not a scratch. We were lucky. But how strange."

"Move a little closer," he said softly. "I think I can make you feel better. Much better."

I giggled and pounced on him. "OK, wise guy. Prove it!"

At noon I walked over to Front Street and arrived just as Melanie was driving up.

"Aunt Ruby was so mysterious," Melanie said. "She insisted we come here for lunch today. Two days until the wedding and with all we have to do. She said Binkie would not be here, and that we had to talk. She wouldn't take no for an answer."

"You know, Mel, just the other day you were complaining that she was unavailable. Remember? You were convinced she was sick. I sure hope that is not what all of the mystery is about? And where's Binkie? He's been scarce too."

Melanie had found a place to park a half block from Binkie's cute little bungalow and we had walked together to his front door. He had inherited the house from his mother. After he and Aunt Ruby married, they divided their time between his house here and the Chastain family home in Savannah. But the soaring poverty and crime rate in Savannah had finally gotten to Aunt Ruby and she donated the house to the city, feeling that they had a better chance of keeping the vandals and the homeless at bay than she.

"I know when I've been beaten," she had said about her efforts to preserve our family home in a hostile environment.

I rang the bell at the Front Street house.

Aunt Ruby opened the door immediately as if she had been standing on the other side. "Hello, my dears," she said. "Come in. Come in." And she gave us each a warm embrace.

"Aunt Ruby, you're looking well," I said, and gave Melanie a meaningful look that was meant to say: See, she's not ill. She was dressed in a royal blue dress with a double strand of pearls and pearl earrings. With low-heeled black patent leather pumps, she looked as if she were dressed for church or lunch at the country club. Aunt Ruby colored her hair, a light warm brown. I'd never seen a strand of gray.

"Come on back to the parlor. I've made sandwiches and iced tea. And we have a guest."

I followed her down the narrow hallway with Melanie at my heels and into the parlor which was decorated exactly as Binkie's mother had left it: nice mahogany antiques, faded chintzes on the Chippendale pieces, and down-filled plump cushions.

Aunt Ruby's guest sat perched on the edge of the sofa. The look she gave us was speculative. And apologetic. It cried out: Please approve of me.

Melanie's mouth dropped open as she faced the woman and it was like she was looking into a mirror. Then, hands on hips, she demanded angrily, "Who the hell are you? And why are you impersonating me?"

"I'm sorry if I startled you," Melanie's look-alike said.

"Melanie, mind your manners," Aunt Ruby said firmly. "She is not impersonating you. Why would she? She is who she is."

"And exactly who is that?" Melanie demanded.

"Look," Aunt Ruby said, "let's all sit down, and calm down. I'll explain everything."

We were raised to mind and respect our elders so we chose our chairs and sat and waited for Aunt Ruby to explain. But I couldn't help staring at the stranger in my aunt's parlor.

"Ashley. Melanie. I don't know quite how to put this. There is no good way. So please, prepare yourselves for a bit of a shock. This is Scarlett Barrett. She is your mother's daughter. She is your step-sister."

"What!" Melanie and I screeched together. We were so shocked we each flung out a hand to grab the other's, clutching for support.

"It's true," Aunt Ruby continued. "And I am so sorry to break it to you this way, but there was no easy way to tell you."

"Ashley, Melanie," Scarlett said soothingly, "I know it must be hard for you to have me sprung on you out of the blue. But it is the truth. I am your older half-sister. I have always wanted to meet you, but Auntie Claire said you didn't know about me, that it would . . ."

"Auntie Claire said!" Melanie exclaimed bitterly. "Our mama? Our mama discussed us with you?"

"Why yes, Melanie, she did. Now please don't be upset. I didn't come here to upset you."

"Well then, why did you come here? Have you been skulking around? Have people seen you? I have a reputation to maintain. So does Ashley."

"I have not been skulking! I came to see Aunt Ruby because we had so much to discuss, catching up to do. And also because I wanted to get to know you. Both of you.

"I wasn't able to find Aunt Ruby in Savannah. She did not live at the old house. It has been years since we last saw each other. But I did see your wedding announcements in the Savannah newspaper two Sundays ago and drove here immediately."

"And just when did you see our mama?" I asked. "And where?"

Melanie crossed her arms over her chest in a defensive posture, and sat up even straighter in the faded chintz wing chair. "Yes, where? Were you sneaking around here while we were growing up?"

Scarlett gave Aunt Ruby a helpless look. "I was afraid I'd

get this reaction. I told you this wouldn't work. I'll go." She got up to leave.

"No!" Aunt Ruby cried sternly. "You will not go. You've none nothing wrong, and you are entitled to respect from these girls. Ashley, Melanie, I'm ashamed of you girls. And your mama would be too. She raised you better. Melanie Wilkes, you mind your manners. You too, Ashley. Now sit back down, Scarlett."

9

Scarlett resumed her seat on the sofa next to Aunt Ruby and Aunt Ruby reached out her arm and gave Scarlett a comforting hug. Then she told us, "Do you remember how your mother used to make trips to New York twice a year? That is where Scarlett grew up. Your mother used to visit her there. Your mother loved all three of you girls but she was trying to preserve her marriage to your father and trying to protect you girls from what she saw as a weakness in her past."

"Aunt Ruby, please," I said. "Start at the beginning and tell us the whole story. Scarlett, I'm sorry if we've been rude to you. You look just like Mama. And Melanie. It's been quite a shock."

Melanie joined in. "Yes, a shock to have you show up, and right when we're already stressed out over the wedding. Sorry."

But I knew Melanie well enough to know that she was not feeling contrite, but acting nice, the way we'd been raised to act. How many times had I heard Mama say to us, "Be nice, girls," when we were acting up as youngsters?

"All right," Aunt Ruby began as she reached for the iced tea pitcher to fill our glasses. "I'll tell you some ancient history. But first, help yourselves to a sandwich. It'll do you good to have some nourishment in your stomach.

"Now," she began after a sip of tea. She seemed nervous, and Aunt Ruby was impervious to nervousness. I'd never seen her nervous before. She cleared her throat.

"When Claire was seventeen she fell in love with a Savannah boy named Rickie Barrett. A nice boy. From a nice family. Our mama and daddy did not object to him, but they were troubled that Claire was so young. She and Rickie were as thick as grits. Inseparable. The Vietnam War was at its height and Rickie, who was twenty at the time, was in the R.O.T.C. Well, he got called up, and it just about tore Claire apart. He was shipped to Vietnam and your mama cried herself to sleep for months.

"Six months after he departed, his parents, Eugene and Jo Barrett, got a visit from two army officers. Rickie had been killed in an ambush by the Viet Cong. Claire was hysterical. Daddy sent for the doctor. She had to be medicated but they had to be careful because she was six months pregnant."

"Oh, lord," Melanie murmured.

"Your grandmother Chastain decided it was time for a prolonged visit to her family in Richmond and that Claire must accompany her. And you, Scarlett, were born in Richmond. There was never any thought of giving you up to strangers. Right away, Eugene and Jo claimed you for their own. They said you were all they had left of Rickie who had been an only child."

"My mother told me everything," Scarlett said in a subdued voice. "She told me how heartsick she had been. How grief stricken."

"She was clinically depressed, Scarlett," Aunt Ruby said. "It was bad. She was that way for years. And she didn't come out of it until she met Peter Wilkes. She told me she had never told him about you. She said that at first she was afraid he'd think badly of her, and then later, it seemed too late, that if she told him then, it would seem that she had been lying to him and misrepresenting herself. So she didn't tell him. Never told him."

Scarlett spoke next as Melanie and I listened intently. "I grew up in the heart of New York City. My daddy – that's how I thought of him, but he was really my grandfather – was an executive with a large chemical company. Mother, that is Grandmother Jo, occupied herself with charities. She was a wonderful mother to me. They both were wonderful parents. They talked about how much it hurt to lose their only son and that if it were not for me they would have died of grief. I was a blessing, they told me, and they loved your mother for giving me to them.

"I knew they were my grandparents but since they were the only mother and father I ever knew, I didn't think much of it. I didn't know anything else."

"I was happy. I attended a private girls' school. I had many friends. I was popular. And music was my life. Voice lessons and piano lessons. Dancing lessons. First ballet, then modern dance. I loved precision dancing and eventually I landed a role with the Rockettes, performing at Radio City Music Hall and on tour. So you see I had a full and happy life until something happened to spoil everything almost six years ago."

"When did you meet our mother?" I asked, more interested in Scarlett's relationship with our mother than in Scarlett's problems.

"I've always known her, ever since I was a little girl. I grew up knowing her but we called her Auntie Claire. Mother would say, 'Auntie Claire's coming for a visit, Scarlett,' and we'd all be excited and pleased to see her. She showed us pictures of her babies, and I remember how happy my mother and daddy were for her. And relieved; they seemed relieved. Later, I figured out that they must have worried that Claire would one day try to reclaim me."

"I remember those shopping trips," Melanie said. "I never understood why she refused to take me with her. But Daddy said she needed time to herself. Mama was always kind of fragile, you know. And I thought he was right, because she always seemed happier when she returned home."

Melanie got a thoughtful look on her face. "Always seemed happier? It was seeing you that made her happy."

"Auntie Claire was so proud of you girls and told us all about your latest accomplishments. About Ashley's artistic abilities, and Melanie's cheer leading, and when you won the North Carolina beauty pageant – why, she was simply over the moon!"

"Mama used that expression all of the time," I said. "She

always used to say that something was 'simply over the moon'."

Melanie turned to Aunt Ruby. "Were you in touch with her too?"

"Yes, dear. I stayed in touch with the Barretts until their deaths. And then about six years ago, I lost touch with Scarlett. Her phone had been disconnected, the condo had been sold, and I simply could not find her. I was very concerned. Scarlett, dear, I have missed you so much."

"Me too, Aunt Ruby. I'm glad we are reunited. And we'll make up for the years we've been apart."

"Then, Scarlett, I guess you didn't know when Mama died almost a year and a half ago," Melanie said. "Aunt Ruby would not have been able to reach you to tell you. I'm sorry you could not come to the funeral."

"And your name," I interjected. "How like Mama to call you Scarlett. You know, I've always wondered why she had not given Melanie the name of Scarlett. She was so smitten with the *Gone With the Wind* characters."

Scarlett smiled a sad little smile, and her smile was so like Melanie's. And Mama's. "You are right. Aunt Ruby was not able to reach me to tell me about my mother's death."

For a second I was jolted. It was jarring to hear this stranger refer to my mother as her mother.

Scarlett went on, "But I did know when she died. I learned about her death from *Star-News* online. Circumstances prevented me from being here. It was impossible for me to come," she said sadly. "I wanted to be here. And it about broke my heart that I couldn't be."

Again, Aunt Ruby covered Scarlett's hand with her own. "It would have been dangerous for Scarlett to attend the funeral. Tell them, Scarlett. Tell them everything."

10

Aunt Ruby turned to us. "She's been staying here with Binkie and me. We have talked and talked, and finally caught up. Now it is your turn to hear her story."

"This is all so mysterious," Melanie said.

Scarlett began, "Almost six years ago something happened that changed the course of my life drastically. And not for the better. I am lucky to be alive."

"What happened?" I asked.

"Yes, tell us what happened," Melanie said.

"It's a long and complicated story and it happened all because I foolishly kept a car in Manhattan. Nobody drives in Manhattan. It's just plain foolhardy . . ."

"Foolhardy!" I interrupted. "That's another one of Mama's expressions."

"Ashley, don't interrupt," Melanie scolded.

"Oh, sorry, Scarlett. Please go on with your story."

"I inherited our apartment from my parents. And Daddy

left me a sporty little BMW that he loved to drive around Manhattan on weekends, or take out into the country, and 'open her up' as he would say. I could have sold the car, but like Daddy I enjoyed driving her occasionally. And as our condominium on Beekman Place was in a large apartment house with an underground garage, parking was not a problem. But mostly I took buses or cabs."

Aunt Ruby got up. "I think we'll be needing something stronger than iced tea. I've got a nice bottle of Harvey's Bristol Cream that I've been saving. Let me open that."

While we waited for Aunt Ruby to return with a tray of glasses and the bottle, and a crystal plate of lemon wedges, Scarlett told us that her parents had died of illnesses, one shortly after the other.

"It happens that way in a good marriage," I said. "Our mama went downhill after Daddy died. She never was the same."

"I'm sorry I didn't know," Scarlett said. "We were all old enough by then for us to finally know one another. And we would have if it were not for what happened that night six years ago."

Melanie moved to the edge of her seat. "What happened?" she asked as Aunt Ruby handed us each a glass of sherry.

"It was a Saturday night. I was dancing in the eight o'clock performance at the music hall. Then there was a party at the apartment of one of the cast. I knew it was going to be a late night so I took the BMW.

"After the show, I filled the car with as many of my

friends from the cast as would fit and we drove further uptown to the party. I parked on the street. At about one o'clock, I'd had enough and left the party — alone.

"I took Fifth Avenue downtown. Someone had set a partially-full Coca-Cola can on the floor and it rolled over and was spilling onto the carpet. Now Daddy had kept that car in pristine condition and I prided myself on doing the same.

"So when I spotted a bus stop on the Central Park side of Fifth Avenue, I pulled over to the curb. I was in the lower Sixties by then, just below the children's zoo and before you reach the Grand Army Plaza. There's a high stone wall that separates the park from the sidewalk, but there are entrances into the park spaced at intervals. No one goes into the park at night."

"Oh gosh, Scarlett, you are really spooking me out," Melanie said.

"Me too," I said, remembering my days as a student in New York. I sipped sherry; it was hot and cold at the same time. Cold on my tongue, yet hot on the back of my throat. I needed that warmth. Bad news was coming, I was sure of it, and I remembered Kiki's reading of the cards. The Queen of Cups signified conflict, aggression, a struggle. Was Scarlett the Queen of Cups? It seemed that she was the mysterious woman whom it was up to me to identify.

Scarlett continued, "I parked at the curb and opened the driver's side door to spill the Coca-Cola out onto the pavement. I had to put the car into park so I could open the door. The doors lock automatically when you are in drive, you see, but when you are in park, they unlock automatically too."

"Oh, no," I gasped. I had lived in New York for four years: you did not drive around with unlocked car doors.

Scarlett continued, "Before I knew what was happening a man had jumped into the car on the passenger side. I thought it was a car jacking. I told him I'd get out. The keys were in the ignition. I told him he could have the car. Just let me go.

"But he made it plain he wanted both me and the car. He had a gun which he pressed against my temple and he ripped the keys out of the ignition. He said, 'Now we're going for a walk, girlie, or I'll shoot you dead right here and now.' And here's another foolish thing. I didn't even have my seat belt on. That might have bought me some time.

"With brute strength he dragged me over the stick shift and out through the passenger door. At that time I was in good shape, better than I am now. I was strong but I was no match for him. I realized that he had size and male strength on his side, that fighting him would be hard."

"Gosh, that must have hurt, to be dragged across the stick shift," I said.

"My adrenalin was pumping so hard I didn't feel a thing. My mind kept racing. Assessing the possibilities. Scream, I thought, and I did. But there was no one around. It was about one thirty a.m. by then. Even the late-night dog walkers were indoors. Away in the distance I could see a doorman in a green uniform, swinging his arms and pacing, but he was too far away, and with the background noise of the city, he didn't hear me.

"If any of the drivers on Fifth Avenue saw me they didn't stop. Maybe they didn't know that I was being forced against my will."

"And he had a gun at your head," Melanie said and rubbed her upper arms as if she was cold.

"The only thing I could do was scream, so I did, at the top of my voice," Scarlett went on. "That made him mad and he struck me on the head with the butt of the gun and I blacked out. When I woke up I was in the park, lying on a rocky outcropping with the man on top of me ripping at my clothes."

11

"Oh, no, I was afraid you were going to say that," I said.

"Poor Scarlett," Aunt Ruby said. But she already knew the story.

"I was so scared. At the same time I was outraged. He was heavy, and ragged and he smelled dreadful. His smell just about made me sick to my stomach. And the thought that that awful creature wanted to enter my body, well, it just made me as mad as the dickens."

"Another one of Mama's saying," I couldn't help but remark.

"Shush," Melanie said. "What happened next, Scarlett? I hope you got away."

"I felt around on that rocky ledge until I found a loose rock. By that time he was kind of straddling my legs, and yanking at my jeans. But my hands were free and I had some breathing room. I picked up that rock and I let him have it. Smashed it as hard as I could against his head."

"Good for you!" I cried. "I'd have done the same. Nobody messes with us Wilkes girls. Let me correct that: nobody messes with Claire's girls."

Scarlett smiled. She got my meaning. She was being accepted. Somehow this dreadful story was endearing her to me. And was Melanie softening too? Aunt Ruby approved of her and wanted her in our lives. And Aunt Ruby had excellent judgment.

Scarlett continued, "Well, then he fell on me. And he was so darned heavy I couldn't push him off me. Finally, I managed to wiggle out from under him. And I started to run off that ledge and through the shrubbery when suddenly I realized he had the keys to my car. And I remembered that when we left the car I'd heard the little beep that meant he had clicked the remote and locked the doors. Should I just leave them? My purse was in the car. I'd have to flag down a motorist on Fifth Avenue. Or find that doorman and get him to call the police.

"Then I reasoned that when the man came to, he'd get my car and my purse with my address and my house keys.

"And at that point I wasn't sure I wanted any police involvement. That dreadful man had not succeeded in raping me. I just wanted to get home and have a bath, and wash his stench off me."

"So you returned for the keys," Melanie guessed.

"I returned for the keys," Scarlett said. "I saw the gun lying next to him. He was out cold. I picked up the gun and trained it on him. But he did not wake up as I went through his pockets – oh, it was odious just to touch him. But I located my car keys.

"Then I jumped up and took off and I took the gun with me. I reasoned that I didn't know what kind of characters I might encounter in that scary park."

"Good thinking," I said.

"I ran through the underbrush and found the footpath. I could see the towers of Fifth Avenue all lit up and I ran toward them. I didn't see a soul. But then as I rounded a bend I came upon two men standing next to a park bench. They were directly under a street lamp so I could see them clearly. Both men were dressed in formal clothing, tuxedoes, as if they had been to a fancy party. I remember that in the murky light of the street lantern, their shirt fronts appeared glistening white. And one man was wearing white gloves. In the garish lamplight they appeared an eerie blue.

"They didn't see me. They were fighting with each other, grappling, and slugging each other. The man with the gloves was larger and more powerful. I stopped and hid behind some foliage. Then the man with the white gloves had the other man by the neck. He was choking the life out of him. The victim was struggling to get free, trying to pull his attacker's hands away from his neck."

"Oh, no," I gasped.

"The victim's legs buckled. He was going down. But his assailant still had him by the neck, squeezing, and yelling at him something about how no one was selling him out.

"At that point, I couldn't take any more. I just ran. I have strong legs from dancing, and I was in good shape. I was a swift runner.

"I flew right past them. The man who was choking the

other was surprised to see me, but he did not let go of his victim. I kept running. And I was holding the gun and pointing it straight at him.

"Then, as I got closer to Fifth Avenue, I felt him following me. I heard his footfalls as he chased me. I looked around and there he was, gaining on me. I put on a burst of speed and escaped through the park exit, dashed across the sidewalk and ran out into the street, around my car. Used the remote to unlock the doors and jumped inside. I pulled away from the curb so fast I skidded. I didn't even bother to look to see if there were cars coming. I just raced down Fifth, not even stopping for the red light.

"But when I was pulling away from the curb, I caught sight of him in my rear view mirror and I knew he was getting my license plate number."

"Then what happened?" I asked, now on the edge of my chair like Melanie. "Did you go to the police?"

"Yes, I went straight to the police. I was bruised and scraped. My head was throbbing where I'd been pistol whipped, and my left eye was swollen almost shut. But I drove straight to the Seventeenth Precinct which is in my neighborhood, on Fifty-First Street near Third Avenue.

"I double parked and ran inside. The desk sergeant took one look at me and led me straight to the back to the detectives. They took a brief statement, then sent for a doctor who cleaned up my scrapes and gave me a cold pack for my forehead.

"After the doctor left, I told the detectives every detail of what had happened. Oh, and of course I turned the gun over to them. I thought they might be able to trace it to my attacker.

"Right away they sent out a team of detectives and uniformed officers to the park. One of the detectives stayed with me, and gave me the mug book to go through. But I didn't recognize anyone."

"So when they found the strangling victim, was he still alive?" I asked.

Scarlett shook her head negatively and gave me an odd look. "They did not find him. When they returned, they said it had been a wild-goose chase. There was no victim on the footpath. They said they'd comb the park in the morning when it was daylight. But I could tell they didn't believe me. They did not find my abductor either. All three men had disappeared. Without a trace."

12

"What about the gun? That was proof," Melanie said.

Scarlett responded, "At that point I was getting the impression they thought I was lying. That the gun was mine. They started questioning me in an aggressive way. I yelled at them, 'Do you think I hit myself on the head?'"

"How strange," I said.

"They must have done a background check on me because they seemed to know a lot about me. One of the detectives said he'd taken his family to the Christmas show at the music hall so he'd probably seen me dance. They were not disrespectful. Just not believing.

"Hearing that I'd been coming home from a cast party, one even asked if there had been drugs at the party."

"No!" I said.

"I told them firmly that I did not do drugs. Drugs and dancing don't mix. Plus, I've never even been tempted. I've seen drugs destroy too many promising careers."

"So what happened next?" Melanie asked.

"I told them that the killer may have gotten my license plate number. That he might be able to trace it and find me. That I was in jeopardy. The older detective, the one who had seen me dance, said that since there wasn't any crime, there was nothing they could do. He suggested I stay with a friend."

"Did you?" I asked.

"Not that night. I drove home. It was almost four in the morning. I parked the car in the underground garage. You need a card to get into the garage so I thought I'd be OK for the rest of the night . . . morning. I turned on the alarm system, had a long soak in the tub, then slept until noon.

"I didn't have a performance the next day, but when I returned from rehearsals, the doorman told me that a man had been looking for me."

"No!" I said. "He did trace you."

"I packed up my stuff, set the alarm on the apartment, and took a cab to my best friend Maggie's apartment. I told her everything. She had a brother who was a cop and he made some inquiries. It hadn't come out in the papers yet, but the word was a New York City Councilman was missing!"

"What?" I exclaimed.

"The councilman had disappeared the same night I'd witnessed that slaying in the park. At that point I didn't know what to do. Should I call the detectives again, I wondered. As it turned out, I didn't have to do anything. The next day I got a phone call at work from a man who said he was an FBI agent. He insisted that we meet.

"I didn't know who to trust. Maybe he was the killer, trying to trick me. I set up a meeting at Maggie's apartment with her cop brother Joe there for protection."

"And was he legit? Was he FBI?" I asked.

"Yes, and there were two of them, a man and a woman. They had IDs that seemed right. The agents wanted me to go downtown with them, but I refused. So we went into Maggie's study and closed the door, with Maggie and Joe stationed nearby in the living room in case I needed them. After we talked for a while, I knew they were who they said they were."

"How did you know?" I asked.

"They showed me more pictures. And this time the strangler was among them. I had no trouble identifying him. Besides, I'd never forget that face. I still see it in the middle of the night when I can't sleep. Cold and sneering. Sort of smug looking. And very dangerous in appearance. Like just a look from him would stop you dead in your tracks.

"They also showed me a picture of the victim. I verified that he was the man I'd seen being strangled. They informed me he was Councilman Henry Falco. His body had been found at a construction site early the morning before. He'd been strangled and kicked savagely."

"But how did the FBI get involved? How did they find you?" Melanie wanted to know.

"I assumed they learned from the Seventeenth Precinct detectives that there had been a woman who claimed to have witnessed a murder in the park. The FBI had been handling an investigation of Falco. Extortion, accepting bribes, awarding contracts to friends, corruption in government. But it seems Falco had friends in high places who wanted him to run for the U.S. House of Representatives. So Falco had to clean up his act. He made a deal with the FBI that he'd provide information about a racketeer named Blackie Sullivan in exchange for anonymity. He would not be charged or investigated if what he gave them was useful. He would not have to testify. The FBI would simply take the information he provided, and use it to find other informers and to build a case."

"Who is Blackie Sullivan?" Melanie asked.

"Russell Sullivan, the man I identified as the strangler. Head of a criminal syndicate that controlled the building trade unions and who had their greedy fingers into all aspects of construction in New York City. Compared with what they wanted to get on Sullivan, the FBI was willing to let Falco and his petty bribes take a walk. He was just one of many who had taken bribes from Sullivan.

"They granted Falco immunity from prosecution. His involvement would be kept secret. You won't believe how corrupt the whole system is. Falco could still run for the U.S. Congress. The public would never know about his shady dealings. His deposition would be sealed."

"Well, if he was an informer, why did he meet with Blackie Sullivan?" I asked. "Didn't he know he'd be in danger?"

Scarlett shrugged her shoulders, a gesture I'd seen Melanie perform countless times. "I asked the agents that question myself. They said: You know what those politicians are like. *Hubris*. Arrogant. Full of themselves. Think they are God's gift to the world and nothing can touch them.

"Falco suggested one last sting. He figured if he could

hand them Sullivan on a silver platter, they'd be so grateful they'd stay off his back forever.

"The agents thought it was a dumb move on Falco's part, but he insisted. The agents implied that Falco wasn't very smart. And that being put up as a candidate for Congress had gone to this head. He thought he was untouchable. He wouldn't be the first to overrate himself, they said."

"Out-smarted himself, that's for sure," Aunt Ruby interjected.

"That was supposed to be the last sting. He was wearing a wire. There was a big fund raiser at the Plaza Hotel that night and both Falco and Sullivan were on the guest list. So Falco was supposed to lure Sullivan away from the party and record him on tape offering a bribe to a city official."

"And did he? Did Sullivan offer him a bribe?" I asked.

"We'll never know. The tape was not found on Falco's body."

"So Sullivan was onto him," I said.

"On TV, the feds are always stationed nearby listening to the conversation from a parked van," Aunt Ruby said.

"I know. I expressed the same disbelief. Falco insisted they stay away. He said Blackie was too slick, had too many contacts, and Falco didn't want to take the chance of Sullivan being onto him."

"But Sullivan was onto him despite his precautions," Melanie said.

"Yes. His plan was to tape the conversation and then turn the tape over to the agents. And they went along with him because Sullivan was a fish the FBI really wanted to fry.

"Only then Falco was dead and the tape was missing," Scarlett concluded.

"But now they had a murder charge on Sullivan!" I exclaimed.

"And an eye witness. You," Melanie added.

"Here's something I don't understand, Scarlett," I said. "Why did Blackie strangle the councilman? Why not just shoot him? If he was planning to kill him, he would have brought a weapon, wouldn't he?"

"There was a lot of speculation about that," Scarlett replied. "It was assumed that because he was wearing a tuxedo he might not have been able to conceal a weapon easily. It might have bulged. Then too, one of the agents said, he might have not wanted to leave behind any evidence, and they can trace bullets to guns. He wore gloves; so no fingerprints. Only white lint. And that is too common. He was clever."

Melanie asked, "What happened next?"

"Well, it was clear that I was valuable to them. And it was clear to me that I was in grave danger. I'd never be able to perform in public again. I'd have to give up my dancing career. Sullivan and his mob would find me and silence me."

"Oh no," I said, figuring it out.

"Oh no, what?" Melanie asked, all hyper.

"Witness Protection!" I declared. "They put you in Witness Protection, didn't they?"

"Yes," Scarlett replied with a long sigh.

"That's why we couldn't find you," Aunt Ruby said. "Your mother was so upset and worried."

Scarlett went on, "I couldn't tell anyone, Aunt Ruby, or I'd be exposing you to the threat too. My life as I knew it was over. And I remained in Witness Protection ever since. All the while the FBI was building a solid case against Sullivan. Murder, racketeering, corruption, bribery, and unsafe construction practices that resulted in the deaths of innocent people when buildings collapsed."

"But why didn't they just charge him with murder, based on your eye witness report?" Melanie asked.

"A slick lawyer would have gotten him off. He could have made me out to be a not credible witness. Dark night, poor lighting. A girl coming home late from a theatre party where there were probably drugs. You know what theatre people are like, he'd tell the jury with a shrug. Then claiming she'd been assaulted. Upset, not thinking coherently. Seeing things. Plus, Sullivan could have claimed it was self defense. No. They wanted to use my testimony as just one more building block in the case they were building against Sullivan. And as it turned out, they did finally prosecute him in federal court. I did testify against him. He is locked away for life. No chance for parole. He'll die in a federal prison. They put him out of business, and his gang too, lock, stock and barrel."

13

The bridesmaids, even the married ones, and the female guests swarmed around Ray like bees at a honeycomb. The moment he appeared on the porch at the top of the Bellamy mansion's impressive one hundred and fifty year old front staircase, he caused a flutter in every woman's heart. Ray is that handsome! He looks a lot like Kiki. But the features that make Kiki appear exotic and a bit fearsome make Ray look irresistible and approachable. His lips are full; his eyes are dark chocolate brown, almost black, large and liquid. A girl would like to lose herself in those eyes. And those arms. He is a big man but not in an intimidating way, more like in a teddy-bear way. Cuddily. Very approachable.

And he is rich! And I'm sure that fact had raced around Wilmington with all the speed of a NASCAR entry. At twenty-seven he is one of the youngest richest men in America.

"There you are, you sweet thing," Melanie cried, and somehow managed to squirm her way through the bevy of admirers and maneuver herself under Ray's left arm so that it looked like he had just wrapped his arm around her. A waiter came by with a tray of red wine and Ray snagged a glass for himself.

I scanned the mansion's front porch for Cam, hoping he was not seeing this little bit of live theatre involving his wanton bride-to-be. One night of freedom remained, and it looked like Melanie was going to make the most of it.

Through the open front doors I spotted Cam in the large reception hall, getting a lecture from his mother. Poor Cam. He was just too nice. Yet he was an industry leader, had stood up to state legislators and made it in a field where the competition was cut-throat. He was not a wimp. Still, it seemed that where women were concerned, he was a pushover. Too passive and conciliatory. Guess that came from being raised by Nelda.

Cam had not seen Melanie with Ray, and I hoped to avoid that. I moved into the circle surrounding Ray, squeezed in at Ray's other side and said, "Ray, have you met Kelly Lauder?"

Kelly was a New York supermodel who had grown up here in Wilmington, and had been Melanie's best friend in high school. Kelly had long blonde hair worn up in a pony tail, and she was wearing a black wrap dress that showed off her figure.

"I was about to introduce them," Melanie said in a miffed voice, "but you beat me to it."

Ray moved his left arm away from Melanie, transferred his wine glass to his left hand, and extended his right hand to Kelly. "Kelly, we met one night at the intermission of *La Boehme*. But I don't expect you remember me."

Ray was not only rich and a hunk, he was also genuinely modest.

"Of course, I remember you, Ray," Kelly said, and gave him one of her wide-eyed doe-like gazes. Whenever a man came around, Kelly turned up the voltage. Her gestures and body language shouted: Look at me! I'm a super model. Just look at my long mane of pale blonde hair. Just see my long sleek legs, and my high, full breasts. And being a man, and guileless, Ray did not fail to notice.

Neither did Melanie. And neither did the other girls. They reached out their hands to Ray and introduced themselves.

"I'm Crystal Lynne, sugar pie," Crystal Lynne said in a sugary Southern accent. Crystal Lynne is a beauty as well, having been runner-up when Melanie was crowned Miss North Carolina. "And I'm looking forward to treating y'all to some of our down-home Southern hospitality."

One of Willie Hudson's granddaughters was there as well, a stunning young woman who was tall and stately. She was the only one of the girls who could look Ray squarely in the eyes. And she did. A long, languid look.

He can have any one of them, I thought, or all of them. Including Melanie. Just how far had this flirtation gone, I asked myself.

I slipped away and into the reception hall. "Cam," I called with fake cheer. "Let's go into the parlor and check out the *hors d'oeveres*. You too, Nelda," I added and didn't have time to wonder if I had been discourteous.

"Let's see what Elaine has prepared for us. And have you seen the grooms' cake?"

I steered them into the main parlor, chattering all the while. "Nelda, let me tell you about the mansion."

She gave me a snooty look which seemed to say, Must you?

"This mansion is a spectacular example of antebellum architecture — a mixture of Greek Revival and Italianate styles. It was built in 1859 by Dr. John D. Bellamy, a wealthy planter. When Wilmington fell to Federal troops, the Union General Joseph Hawley commandeered the house as his headquarters. But then after the war ended, Hawley refused to return the house to Dr. Bellamy. So Bellamy went to Washington to personally petition President Andrew Johnson for the return of his house. And he got it back."

"A charming, provincial tale, I'm sure," Nelda said.

"It is fascinating, Mother," Cam said, "to live with all of this history surrounding us. One of the reasons I feel in love with Wilmington. And of course you know the other reason. Where is she?" And he searched the parlor with his eyes.

"She's probably out back with Elaine at Elaine's catering van. You know how hands-on Melanie is. She doesn't leave anything to chance."

But Nelda stayed on focus. "Now Cam, darling, there is nothing like living in Italy if one wishes to be surrounded by history." She laid a hand on his arm. And ignoring the fact that I was there and able to hear her every word, she asked, "Are you absolutely sure you want to stay here? Are you sure you don't want to return to Italy with me? It isn't too late to back out of this . . . this commitment?"

Wow, this lady was nervy. I would have been totally outraged if it were not for the fact that Melanie was misbehaving herself.

Nelda turned and looked toward the veranda. "From what I saw a moment ago, it doesn't seem to me that your fiancé will be alone for long if you cancel this foolish wedding."

I gasped. Foolish wedding!

Cam seemed to tune her out and only turned to look where Nelda pointed. But by that time, Melanie and Ray had disappeared from view leaving behind a group of beautiful but disappointed admirers.

Oh, Melanie, when I get my hands on you I am going to wring your neck.

I grabbed Nelda's hand away from Cam's arm. "Just look, Nelda, these are the original brass chandeliers, originally gas lights at one time. And don't you just love the way they've carpeted the rooms with these colorful Victorian carpets? People think the Victorians went in for drab colors. Not so."

Nelda was now looking at me as if I had gone mad. And had I?

"Let's get something to eat," I said desperately. When all else fails, go for food.

Scarlett came rushing by and she was crying. Now what?

"And just see the chocolate grooms' cake. We're going to toast the grooms later." I was blabbing. Where had Melanie gone?

This was our rehearsal dinner and supposed to be a fun event, a festive private party for the wedding party and the out-of-town guests, a relaxing evening before the big day.

And was it? No, neither festive nor relaxing. Not with my sister up to her old tricks. Oh, wait till I get my hands on her.

Then suddenly Jon was at my side and I felt much better. My love, my partner in life, someone to share my worries and my burdens.

He wrapped an arm around my waist and said with a smile, "The rehearsal went well, don't you think? I was so afraid I'd flub my lines, but I didn't." He grinned at Cam and Nelda. "I can't wait until tomorrow when we say them for real."

If there is a wedding tomorrow, I thought to myself. "Jon, can I speak to you alone? Nelda, Cam, will you excuse us? Why don't you try the *hors d'oevres*? They look delicious."

As for myself, I couldn't eat a thing.

14

I led Jon out onto the front porch. "What's wrong?" he asked, moving us over to the railing. In honor of the season, the porch railings and the stair railings had been festooned with green garlands and wrapped with rope lights.

"It's Melanie," I said, furious. "She and Ray slipped away. If Cam finds out what is going on, he'll cancel the wedding, and we won't be having a wedding ceremony tomorrow. Oh, what are we going to do? I'm going to murder my sister."

"Well, let's look around for them. They can't have gone far," Jon suggested.

We descended the front porch stairs and followed a brick sidewalk into the side yard. It was darker here but not so dark we could not see. A few people were mingling here, strolling about on this unseasonably warm evening. But no Ray.

Then suddenly, I saw Melanie, walking away with a man toward the parking lot where there was very little light.

"Melanie!" I called loudly. "Mel!"

She seemed not to hear.

"Melanie!" Jon shouted.

She stopped and turned in our direction. Then she said something to the man and strolled away from him and toward us. When she reached us, she said, "What did you want?"

"What do you mean, 'what did I want'? We just came out to find you."

"I know," she said. "One of the valets said you were looking for me. He said you were out here near the cars. So, what's up?"

I was about to scream. How could she act so innocent? "'What's up? What's up?'" I screeched. "You! You have got to stay away from Ray."

My sister gave me a long level look. "Oh, that Ray is such a honey. I was just trying to fix him up with Kelly. He lives in New York. She lives in New York. They'd be a perfect match, don't you think?"

"Aarrg!" I growled, and turned quickly and stomped off toward the mansion. She was going to deny everything. She was going to spoil everything.

Jon followed. "Ashley, wait up." When he reached me, he said, "Maybe it's not what you think. Maybe she <u>is</u> trying to fix them up."

"Jon, you are so naive. You haven't seen what I've seen."

"I know," he said thoughtfully. "You told me."

We found Scarlett sitting alone at one of the outdoor tables on the veranda. I wanted to have a private word with her. "Jon, would you mind going inside and filling three plates for us?" To Scarlett, I asked, "You haven't eaten yet have you?"

Eyes downcast, she shook her head 'no.'

I turned to Jon, and he got it. He read my expression. I wanted to be alone with Scarlett. "I'll be glad to. Anything special you'd like, Scarlett?"

"No, nothing special. You select. And thanks, Jon."

"I think I saw a platter of those wonderful curried chicken wings that Elaine makes," I said.

As soon as he had gone, I sat down across the table from Scarlett. "You've been crying, haven't you? Would you like to talk?"

"Oh, Ashley, I've lived such a solitary life for so long, now that I'm back in the world, I don't seem to know whom to trust."

She lifted her eyes to me, eyes that were golden green, so much like Melanie's. So much like Mama's. And she looked pretty in a creamy ivory pantsuit with a lacy cammie worn under the jacket.

I reached out and covered her hand with my own. "You know you can trust Aunt Ruby. And you can trust Binkie. And you can trust me. And Melanie."

"Ah, Melanie," Scarlett sighed. "Will she ever accept me, do you think?"

"I think she has, Scarlett. You know, learning about you has served to help us understand our mother. Mama always wore a cloud of sadness about her that try as we might we could not break through. I remember that Melanie and I tried so hard to make her happy. Daddy too, of course. Now I know that it is not the child's job to make the parent happy. We were just kids. If I'm lucky enough to have children, I'll never put them in that position."

"And you think she was grieving over giving me up?" Scarlett asked.

"Yes, I think so. Probably the hardest part was carrying the secret inside her. I know my parents had a good marriage, so I don't know why she did not eventually confide in my dad. He was good guy, and very understanding."

"My dad was too," Scarlett said. "It wasn't a problem for me to be raised by my grandparents. I knew from early on about my biological parents. Auntie Claire came to visit twice a year, and I was surrounded by my father's memorabilia. There were pictures of him in every room of our condo, as a boy, as a man, in uniform. I'm sorry that my mother had such a miserable time of it."

"When she was diagnosed with dementia," I said, "Melanie and I thought that explained some of her odd behavior. Now that we know what was really at the bottom of it, well, it's a help. Scarlett, it has helped Melanie and me to know about you."

Scarlett beamed at me. "Thanks, Ashley, it means a lot to me to hear you say that."

"I just wish we had known about you sooner. If it was fear that my dad would think less of her that prevented her from telling us, why didn't she tell us after he died? He died eight years ago, when I was a freshman at Parson's."

"Maybe by then it had become a way of life for her," Scarlett said.

"You are very wise," I said.

"Perhaps she did get around to wanting to tell you and then later it was too late. I had gone into the Witness Protection program and she couldn't find me," Scarlett suggested.

"Yes, that could be it," I said. "What was it like, living in Witness Protection?"

"Very, very lonely," Scarlett said wistfully. "I couldn't communicate with anyone from the past. You can't imagine how cut off that made me feel. But to do so might put them in danger. And I couldn't make new friends because it was impossible to get close to anyone. Everything about me was a lie. And I missed dancing but I didn't dare risk dancing professionally. That might have led Blackie to me. He had seen my face. He would have found out who I was. And then when I disappeared without a trace, he would have figured out the feds were hiding me."

"So if you didn't dance, what did you do? Where did you live?" I asked.

"I was assigned a U.S. Marshal. He made all of the arrangements for my relocation. They moved me to Phoenix, and enrolled me in a paralegal program at a community college. My new name was Susan Brown. Ha!" she laughed, "not very colorful. I worked at a law firm for five years. My job was very 'behind the scenes'. Safer that way, the marshal told me. I was tucked away in an office. I had no social life to speak of. Maybe dinner with one of the other paralegals every now and then. I couldn't get close to anyone because making up Susan's life was just too difficult and I was afraid of getting caught in a lie and being exposed."

"So you led a very low-profile life," I said. "And after the life of a Rockette that must have been difficult."

"Very difficult, Ashley. I had trouble sleeping, and suffered from migraines. Finally, it was all over. I testified before a Grand Jury about what I had seen that night. The feds had built a solid case against Blackie on additional charges, and there was enough evidence to put him away for the rest of his life. Both parties agreed to a bench trial, that is no jury. I testified there before the judge. He and his gang were sent away."

The party was going on around us, with guests coming and going, but for the moment no one interrupted our conversation. If anyone wondered who this woman was who looked so much like Melanie, they might have assumed she was a cousin. That was how Aunt Ruby had been introducing her.

Scarlett continued her story. "If I thought Witness Protection was a lonely proposition, what I faced after I was returned to my own life was worse. I hadn't danced in six years so there was no hope of asking for my old job with The Rockettes. The government had arranged for the very private, very discreet sale of the New York condo, so although I had money waiting for me in an account, I no longer had a home to return to."

"Oh, Scarlett. I know how I'd feel if I lost my house."

"Thanks for understanding, Ashley. I knew from the obituary in the *Star-News* online that my mother had died. I thought I would find Aunt Ruby. I went to Savannah and discovered that she no longer lived in the Chastain family home, that it was being converted into a museum. I couldn't locate her. Then, a couple of weeks ago, I happened to look at the Society pages and saw the announcement of yours and Melanie's double wedding. I came to Wilmington and found Aunt Ruby. I didn't dare approach you first for fear of shocking you. And well, it was just uncomfortable. I know I've done nothing wrong yet still I feel like the black sheep of this family."

"Scarlett, now listen to me. I want you to stop feeling that way. We are going to introduce you to everyone as our sister. We are going to include you in all our plans. Mama gave you the right name. Scarlett. Your namesake was a plucky, courageous heroine, and so are you!"

15

Our wedding day dawned clear and bright, morning light filtering into the bedroom around the shades. I was too excited to sleep past seven, and quietly left the bed so as not to wake Melanie. We had slept together last night, just like we had many times as little girls. We had talked until midnight. About Scarlett, and Mama and Daddy, and the young soldier Mama had fallen in love with at age seventeen. There had always been a shadow of sadness about Mama and now we knew the reason why.

I didn't have the nerve to confront Melanie about Ray. I was waiting for the right moment.

I peeked out the window to view the day. Nun Street was quiet, still too early for traffic, even on a Saturday morning. Across the street, front doors were festive with red and green wreaths, and porch railings were festooned with colorful swags.

I pulled on my robe, snugged my feet into fuzzy slippers

and tiptoed down the stairs. Wedding day! My wedding day. I hugged myself.

I missed Jon. In keeping with tradition he had slept at his home last night, and Cam had slept at his. But Jon is my best friend and I like to share my feelings and impressions with him, so I missed sharing this sense of elation I was experiencing. Tomorrow, I told myself. After today, we will be together always.

I brewed decaf coffee, a flavor called Death by Chocolate that I buy by the scoop out the bin at Fresh Market. In a few minutes the kitchen smelled like melting chocolate.

As I was pouring my first mug and about to step out onto the kitchen porch to check the temperature, Melanie appeared. I don't know how she does it, but Melanie's hair never gets tangled like mine does when she sleeps. She never looks prune-faced like the rest of us in the morning. She always looks fresh and dewy.

"Hi," I said, filling a coffee mug and handing it to her. "How did you sleep?"

"Like a baby. How's the weather?"

"Let's check."

We went out onto the porch. The air was a bit nippy and the grass was wet but the sun would burn that off soon and warm the air. The Carolina Jessamine that covered the gazebo was in bloom, pretty tiny golden yellow trumpet flowers against narrow, spiky green leaves. The pansies I had planted last month were flourishing, their faces sweet and open and every color imaginable.

I slipped my arm around Melanie's silk-robed waist. "The whole world looks beautiful this morning, doesn't it?"

"Uhmmm," she replied, sipping coffee.

I gave her a long look. "Melanie, you aren't having any regrets are you? You know, your favorite expression used to be, 'the grass is always greener.'"

Melanie gave me a smile. "You are not to worry about me and Cam. Not ever. I know I've been kind of . . . well, let's just say, generous with my favors where men are concerned. But Cam is the only one for me. I'll be true to him. I promised him and I'm promising you. This is one marriage that is going to stick."

"Mine too," I said. "My old life, the part of my life that included Nick, that is all behind me. I have so much to look forward to. And so do you."

Melanie turned back to the house. "We'd better get a move on. I've got calls to make. Elaine's crew and the florist were supposed to be working through the night, setting up the tables in the drawing room at the lodge. Placing the flowers and setting the tables, and decorating the indoor garden room for the 'Kindness Ceremony.'"

"Mel, you know I have only one bathroom so we'll have to take turns in the tub," I said.

"I'm going to have a lovely bubble bath," she said.

"You go first. I'm going to walk around the garden for a bit. I'll see you inside. What time did you say the esthetician was coming?"

Melanie was entering the house and she turned back. "Nine. She'll give us lovely facials. So relaxing."

Then she walked back to my side. "It's going to be hectic today, Ashley, so I may not get a chance to say this." She put her arms around me and gave me a big squeeze. "You were the best baby sister any girl could ask for. I loved you then. And I love you now."

She pulled back with tears sparkling in her bright green eyes. "I'll love you forever. You are going to make a beautiful bride. And you and Jon, Cam and I are going to have a lifetime of fun and adventures."

I was crying now, making little gulping noises in my throat. "Oh, Melanie, I miss Mama and Daddy so much. Wouldn't they be proud?"

"Wouldn't they now?" she echoed. "Somehow I think they know. I think they are watching and giving us their blessing."

"Me too," I said, and squeezed her hard.

Then, laughing, I called after her as she went inside, "Don't use up all the hot water."

I took a turn around my small garden, feeling chilly but the morning air was refreshing and crisp. I needed to talk to God. Why is it so easy to talk to God in a garden? "Bless us, Father," I asked. "Bless our wedding, and bless our marriages. Keep us safe, and free from harm. May your angels surround us today and protect us from the many dangers we mortals face. We are so fragile, yet so strong at the same time. A complex miracle. Your creation."

I bowed my head, made the sign of the cross, and silently wept with happiness.

Then I shook my hair out of my face, squared my shoulders, and marched into the house. I couldn't wait to meet Jon at the church.

16

At ten o'clock Melanie and I were stretched out on adjoining massage tables in my guest room. A relaxing massage before things let loose was her gift to both of us. We had removed our engagement rings and placed them in a dish on the bed table. My ring was a Tiffany style diamond in a platinum band. Very simple but elegant and classic. Melanie's ring was a one a half carat oval cut diamond with white and yellow diamonds set in white gold and yellow gold.

Below us, Spunky was prowling around the tables legs, meowing plaintively, then crouching as if he was tempted to jump up onto Melanie's massage table with her. Spunky is slavish in his devotion to Melanie. He is a cat I rescued two Christmases ago, but the ungrateful beast made eye contact with Melanie one day and wouldn't stop crying until she took him home.

Downstairs, my doorbell rang and Aunt Ruby went down to answer it.

She returned to my bedroom carrying two gift-wrapped boxes. "These just came from the 'Far East and Beyond' antique shop down at Chandler's Wharf. Personally delivered by the shop's owner."

Melanie lifted her head and said, "But we clearly told everyone 'no gifts'."

My masseuse was kneading my feet. "That feels heavenly," I murmured. If she kept this up, I would not be able to get off the table to put on my wedding dress. The ceremony would have to commence without me.

"There are cards," Aunt Ruby said. "This one says, 'Thank you for making my dreams come true. – Cam.' So this box is for you, Melanie."

Gathering the sheet around her, Melanie sat up. "Sorry, Elsie," she told her masseuse.

I sat up too. The other box was for me. Elsie and her partner Abby were wide-eyed. As was I.

I took the second box from Aunt Ruby and read the card silently. "I'm the happiest man in the world. I'll love you forever, Jon." For the second time that day, tears welled up in my eyes.

"I've got to get over this crying jag before the make-up artist does my eyes," I murmured.

Aunt Ruby handed me a tissue. "Open your presents, girls, I can't wait to see what's inside."

"You go first, Mel," I said, watching as she tenderly untied the ribbon. She was going to save the wrappings as a memento. I'd save mine too.

From inside a small flat box, she lifted out a velvet jewelry box. She opened the lid. "Oooooh," she gushed, her mouth gaping. Her eyes lit up like stars. Aunt Ruby and I moved in closer to see.

"A South Seas pearl!" Melanie exclaimed. "I love those pearls." A large gleaming pearl was set in a platinum necklace. "I'll wear it today." She held the box so we could all see. Everyone was exclaiming, ooohing and aaaahing. "That dear Cam. He knows just what I like."

Turning to me, she said, "Open yours, Ashley."

My box was larger. Aunt Ruby helped me unwrap it. "Oh, look, it's a Chinese bridal box!" I said. "Oh, I love it. I'll take it with me on our honeymoon. The bride is supposed to store her valuables in it."

The box was over a hundred years old, made of hand-carved walnut, and set with semi-precious stones. I lifted the lid to find small compartments. And there was a drawer at the bottom that when I drew it out contained more small compartments.

"What will you put in it?" Abby asked.

"I don't know. I'll think of something."

"Where are you going on your honeymoon?" Elsie asked.

"I don't know," I confessed.

"What do you mean, you don't know?"

"Apparently Jon read somewhere that there is an old custom that only the groom knows where he is taking the bride on their honeymoon. I think it must date back to the days when people lived in tribes or something, and in a way the man was stealing the bride away from her tribe. So Jon has planned our honeymoon, and that man is sure good at keeping secrets, because I've begged and he won't even hint."

"How are you supposed to know what to pack?" Elsie asked.

"A good question, Elsie. How will I know?"

"Maybe he's taking you some place where you won't need clothes," Abby said.

We all giggled.

"She wishes," Melanie said, lying back down on the massage table. "I wouldn't let Cam get away with something like that. We're taking his yacht for a long cruise down the coast to Boca. And we're taking that little meowing monster cat with us too. We've both been working very hard and we're looking forward to a relaxing time, lots of dozing in the sun, and going ashore in the evenings for dinner. It will be very romantic."

Any place Jon takes me will be romantic, I thought, because he'll be there. Jon is the most romantic man in the world.

Precious Elaine, our caterer, had thought of everything. She had lunch delivered to my house: turkey and Swiss cheese Panini sandwiches with lettuce and tomato, fruit cups, a variety of sodas and iced green tea.

"I'm glad it just the three of us," I said. "I know, most times the bridesmaids gather with the bride right before the wedding, but this is better. Just us and Aunt Ruby."

"I'm grateful to be standing in for your blessed mother," Aunt Ruby said.

Melanie's cell phone rang. "That's Cam," she said, taking the call and moving from the dining room into the reception hall. "Hello, sweetheart," I heard her say. "Not getting cold feet, are you?" she asked, and her laughter floated back to us.

Aunt Ruby and I exchanged raised eyebrows. Cam get cold feet? Fat chance.

And then my phone rang and I checked the number before answering. Unavailable. Should I pick up? I did. Maybe it was Jon calling from someone's phone.

An unfamiliar male voice said, "Put Scarlett on."

"You must have the wrong number. Scarlett does not live here," I said.

"I know she's there, now put her on."

I closed the phone and cut him off. I looked at Aunt Ruby. "Someone for Scarlett."

"What did he say?" Aunt Ruby asked.

"Not even hello. Just ordered me to put her on."

The doorbell rang again and I went to answer it. I admitted the makeup artists and the hair stylists. My guest room was being used as the dressing room, with our gowns hanging in bags in the closet, and our accessories spread out on the antique rice bed that had been in my mother's family for a hundred years. My great-aunt's rubies that I'd inherited had been retrieved from the safe deposit box at the bank and were waiting to be slipped around my neck.

Then Jon called and I thanked him for the Chinese bridal box and told him I'd cherish it forever and fill it with keepsakes of our life together. "See you soon," I said.

The detritus of luncheon and the mysterious caller forgotten, I followed the others up the stairs to begin our bridal preparations.

17

At three o'clock I was ready. I looked in my cheval looking glass and couldn't believe my eyes. Was that really me? The make-up artist had done a fabulous job on my gray eyes, making them look large and lavender. My hair was piled up on my head in a sophisticated style. Around my neck I wore Great Aunt Lillian's ruby necklace and there were matching tear drop earrings. Not large, just very pretty and warm looking against my dark brown hair.

My dress fit like a dream, hugging my waist which was now trim thanks to Melanie who had restricted my diet with the vigilance of Jenny Craig. The lace bolero jacket we'd had made was the perfect thing to keep my bare arms and shoulders from getting goose bumps.

Melanie came in and we stood side-by-side, admiring ourselves in the mirror. Her auburn hair was upswept as well, held in place with combs that had pearls glued to them. The pearl necklace Cam had sent was beautiful around her neck, and like mine her earrings were teardrops too, but hers were pearls.

Although her dress had cost thousands of dollars, I didn't think it was any prettier than mine which I had purchased off the rack. But I wasn't about to tell her that.

"Your dress is so beautiful," I said and hugged her, careful not to smudge our makeup. Actually, our dresses were very similar, made of white lace over silk, form fitting but flared below the knees. They were both strapless, and the cut of our bolero jackets created the illusion of sweetheart necklines.

"And you look stunning, baby sister," she whispered to me.

"Thanks for not letting me overeat," I whispered back.

She laughed. "See I told you so. What else are big sisters for?"

The doorbell rang again. I went to the top of the stairs. "Nelda Cameron is here," Binkie called up. Nelda's face appeared behind him.

"May I come up? I have 'something old' for both of you to wear."

"Please do come up, Nelda," I called. Was Nelda finally accepting Melanie?

Nelda came into the guest room, carrying two large but flat boxes. She set the boxes on the cluttered bed and hugged both Melanie and me. Then she lifted the lids of both boxes and reached inside to withdraw fine Chantilly lace mantillas.

"These are very old and very precious," she said. "I'd like it if you'd wear them."

Melanie gave me a look. "We'd be proud to wear them.

Right, Ashley?" Anything to be accepted by Cam's mother and to have peace.

Nelda shook out a veil and lifted it onto Melanie's head. From the box, she produced an old-fashioned hatpin with a pearl head and rhinestones. "The hatpins are Victorian," she said.

"That's a large pin," Melanie said, looking at the pin which was about six inches long.

"The Victorian ladies used to wear huge, elaborate hats, and so they needed a long pin like this to secure their hats in place," Nelda said. "This will do fine to secure the mantilla to the curls on top of your head."

Then she helped me arrange my veil, which was not identical to Melanie's but very similar. She secured the veil to the crown of my head where my hair was piled high.

"Don't you girls look like pictures," Aunt Ruby said, and clasped her hands together. "That was a good choice, Nelda. It always bothered me just a little that the girls were getting married bare headed. I think your decision was perfect."

And a friendship was born between the two older women.

Aunt Ruby said, "I think we'd better go. Binkie is wearing out the carpet downstairs."

"I've got a car and driver downstairs," Nelda said. "I'll meet you at the church." And she was gone.

The photographer preceded us down the stairs, snapping pictures as we moved into my reception hall where Binkie was pacing impatiently. "The carriage is here," he said.

"Just look at our girls," Aunt Ruby said to Binkie. "Don't they look lovely?" She blinked back tears.

"They do, indeed," Binkie said emotionally. "And so do you, my dear. You look like a bride yourself."

Aunt Ruby had changed into her formal dress, an elegant red brocade sheath with a matching jacket. Her silk pumps were died to match, and she wore her usual double strand of pearls. The makeup artist had done her makeup as well, and she looked very youthful for a woman in her seventies.

We went out onto the porch and down the stairs, and climbed up into the carriage. For a second I had a fleeting image of another carriage but then the image vanished as quickly as it had come. My neighbors waved to us and we waved back.

The bridesmaids and the guests would be waiting at the church. The photographer snapped several shots of us and the carriage and the horse. Then he got into his car to drive off ahead of us. He had already set up a video camera on the balcony inside the church to capture the guests' arrival and the ceremony.

I had butterflies in my stomach. In just a few minutes I would see Jon.

Our horse was a salt and pepper Percheron draft horse, an unflappable horse who braved the traffic without so much as a flick of the tail. Binkie and I sat in the red plush front seat of the open carriage, Melanie and Aunt Ruby sat in the back seat.

As the carriage rolled gently up Third Street, people on the sidewalks stopped and stared, or waved. And car traffic slowed and the passengers stared at us too.

Our driver, dressed in a black suit with a top hat, waved

and smiled. We must have been a picture in that carriage. The carriage and the horse were decorated with red roses and white ribbons. How often do people see two brides being delivered to the church?

18

Just as we were crossing Ann Street, two men darted out from between parked cars. One of the men grabbed the horse's bridle and brought the horse to a halt as the driver cried, "What are you doing?" But the man trained a gun on the driver and silenced him with a threatening, "Shut up or I'll shoot."

In an instant a second man dashed to the side of the carriage.

There wasn't time to scream. There wasn't time to reach for a cell phone. Besides none of us were carrying cell phones. There was only time to gasp and to try to comprehend what was happening.

A sinister-looking man, a thug, pointed a gun at us and told us not to move. With the speed of a striking snake, he reached up into the carriage and seized Melanie by the arm. She was shrieking and Aunt Ruby was yelling for him to let her go.

"Are you crazy, man?" Binkie yelled.

"Shut up, old man, or I'll start shooting and I don't care which one of youse I hit."

With a hard yank, he pulled Melanie out of the carriage, and she would have fallen onto the sidewalk except that he jerked her to her feet.

She was kicking and screaming.

He held her in front of him, his right hand holding the gun nuzzle against her temple while his free arm encircled her waist.

"You're coming with us, Scarlett," he yelled.

"Are you crazy?" she yelled angrily. "I'm not Scarlett. I'm Melanie Wilkes. Now get your hands off me." And she attempted to jab him with her elbow. He only squeezed her tighter.

"Yeah. That's what you'd like us to think. But I seen your picture in the paper on Sunday. I know who you are. You're the dame that put the finger on Blackie. You ain't getting away with that."

"Do something," I yelled at Binkie. "Somebody do something."

Melanie's arms were free and she reached up and unpinned her veil. The veil went flying off her head, but she had the long hatpin in her hand and before her abductor knew what was happening, she was stabbing the long sharp pin into the hand that held her.

He let out a curse and yanked his arm away from her. She broke free.

Like lightning Binkie jumped up and seized the whip

from its holder. With one quick snap, he brought the whip down onto the man's other arm, causing him to drop the gun.

The man who had been holding the horse's bridle let go. "Let's get outta here," he cried.

Both men turned and ran. But they ran straight into the arms of uniformed police officers who seemed to have appeared from out of nowhere. In seconds the thugs were handcuffed and being led away.

Binkie sprang down from the carriage and helped Melanie back inside.

And then Nick was there, lifting Melanie's veil from the sidewalk and handing it to her.

"Nick! I can't believe you are here. Who were they? What did they want?"

Nick was looking me over with very admiring eyes. "You take a man's breath away, Ashley." Then he composed himself and reverted to his cop's mode. "They are what's left of Blackie Sullivan's gang. We had reports that they were in town, and we've been tailing them. They mistook Melanie for Scarlett Barrett."

"You knew about that?" I asked.

"It's my business to know what is going on in my town, Ashley."

He stepped back and gave me a little salute. "Have a happy life."

Then he waved the carriage on, whisking me away and into my new life with his blessing.

19

The guests were seated. Our wedding party was assembled in the narthex. As Granny Campbell and Nelda Cameron were escorted down the aisle and seated in the first row on the grooms' side, Scarlett stepped to the altar and began singing *Ave Maria* in a clear soprano voice.

The choir door opened and Father Andrew, Jon, and Cameron walked in and took their places at the altar. My heart raced at the sight of Jon.

I had butterflies in my stomach and my palms were sweaty. Then events seemed to proceed quickly and with a power of their own. The organ played Bach's "Jesu, Joy of Man's Desiring" and the five groomsmen trooped down the aisle and lined up on the right side below the altar.

Next came the bridesmaids, looking so pretty in their red gowns with their nosegays of white roses. They were followed by the ring bearer, a sweet lad, the great-grandson of Willie Hudson.

And a precious little girl dressed in a long red dress headed solemnly for the altar, tossing red rose petals onto the aisle runner.

When the organist switched to Beethoven's "Ode to Joy" the guests all stood and turned to look toward the entrance, smiling, expectant, watching for the brides.

"Are you ready?" Binkie asked, taking my left hand and slipping it through his folded arm and then patting my hand gently. His eyes were shiny wet with tears. Mine were too.

"I've waited my whole life for this moment," I responded. "I just didn't know it."

Aunt Ruby was escorting Melanie down the aisle ahead of us and Binkie waited until they were mid-way to the altar before he began his slow even pace. My nosegay of red roses felt light in my right hand.

At the altar Jon waited, light streaming in from a high window illuminating his golden head. He was smiling broadly, his eyes fastened on my face.

I glanced at the guests and smiled but my eyes always returned to Jon. All of a sudden I felt overwhelmingly happy. This was right. So right.

And then a murmur and light laughter came from the congregation and I turned my head to see what had caught their attention. A slight movement behind me made me look back and I laughed out loud.

It was Spunky. Spunky the cat, his white on black patterned fur making him look like he was dressed in a tuxedo. Melanie had tied a red ribbon around his neck. He was following us down the aisle with cat-like grace, ignoring the congregation and the attention he was attracting.

Binkie and I arrived at the altar. He delivered me to Jon and then he and Aunt Ruby took their seats in the front row on the bride's side. Out of the corner of my eye I saw Spunky rolling in the strewn red rose petals. Had catnip been sprinkled with the rose petals? The scent led him to Aunt Ruby's feet. She reached down and scooped him up into her lap, where he draped himself languidly across her knees.

I looked at Melanie and arched my eyebrows. She winked at me and grinned. She was glowing with happiness.

Father Andrew began: "Dearly, beloved: We have come together in the presence of God . . ."

I looked at Jon. He looked at me. We had eyes for only each other.

The priest said, "Ashley, will you have this man to be your husband; to live together in the covenant of marriage? Will you love him, comfort him, honor and keep him, in sickness and in health; and forsaking all others, be faithful to him as long as you both shall live?"

With a glad and thankful heart, I responded, "I will."

The priest said to Jon, "Jonathan, will you have this woman to be your wife . . ."

Looking fully into my eyes, his whole being shining through them, Jon responded, "I will."

Father Andrew repeated the Declaration of Consent with Melanie and Cameron.

Father Andrew then addressed the congregation. "Will all of you witnessing these promises do all in your power to uphold these two couples in their marriages?"

Our guests replied with a resounding and encouraging, "We will."

Father Andrew said, "The Lord be with you."

The congregation replied, "And also with you."

"Let us pray."

After the prayer, Willie Hudson mounted the pulpit and read from Genesis.

Then we two couples exchanged our vows. Jon took my right hand in his and said, "In the Name of God, I, Jonathan Alfred Campbell, take you, Ashley Ann Wilkes, to be my wife, to have and to hold from this day forward, for . . ."

I took Jon's right hand in mine and said, "In the Name of God, I Ashley, take you Jonathan, to be my husband . . ."

Willie's great grandson produced the rings and we slipped our wedding rings on each other's fingers.

We gave ourselves to each other. Father Andrew ended The Marriage with, "Those whom God has joined together let no on put asunder."

And the congregation resounded with a loud, "Amen."

We recited The Lord's Prayer.

Jon and I, Melanie and Cam, knelt at the altar while The Blessing of the Marriage was offered. Then we rose and joyfully participated in The Peace. Jon and I greeted each other as husband and wife. We hugged our attendants and said to each of them, "The peace of the Lord be always with you."

Jon and I and most of the congregation partook of communion. After a last prayer, a trumpeter played Clarke's "Trumpet Voluntary" and the classic trumpet piece filled the sanctuary. Two very happy brides and two very happy grooms, along with our wedding party, trooped down the aisle. On Jon's arm, I know my feet did not touch the carpet. I floated.

So gloriously happy to have given myself to Jon and to have taken him as my darling husband forever more.

20

Outside St. James, the long white stretch limousine waited. Room enough inside for the bridal couples, Aunt Ruby and Binkie, our new sister Scarlett, Nelda, Granny Campbell, and one very mellow cat. As soon as we got in and settled our finery around us, Cam popped the cork on the champagne bottle and filled our fluted glasses from the frothy stream.

"To the happy couples!" Binkie toasted and we clinked glasses.

The others did not know about our perilous carriage ride to the church. "Your hatpin saved Melanie's life, Nelda," I said.

"Isn't that a bit dramatic, dear?" she asked.

With interruptions from Melanie, Aunt Ruby and Binkie, I told them about the harrowing ride when Blackie Sullivan's gang tried to abduct Melanie.

Instantly, Cam was concerned. "Are you all right, love?" he asked.

"Perfect," Melanie replied. "Now. For a moment there it was harrowing. But between my hatpin and Binkie's whip, we sent them flying into the arms of the local police, didn't we, Binkie?"

Binkie grinned. "Correct. We gave them a lesson in how justice is dispensed down here in Rebel Territory."

After that, we had to tell everyone Scarlett's story. That she was not our cousin but our step-sister and that thanks to her a dangerous criminal and his gang had been locked up.

Nelda looked at Scarlett with new respect. "You are a heroine, my dear," she said.

"The wine glass!" I shouted. "It wasn't cracked. It exploded because he was firing a bullet at it," I said. "I'll bet my honeymoon on it."

I looked at Jon and giggled. "I'm sure of it."

"Wouldn't we have heard a gun shot?" Melanie asked.

"Not if he used a silencer. Remember? There were people standing on the pedestrian walkway on the bridge. He could have fired from there," I said.

"I've just realized something else," Melanie said, excited. "At the carriage, the man looked familiar. I thought I had seen him before. Now I remember where. At the rehearsal dinner last night, he posed as a valet and was tricking me into going into the parking lot with him."

"Well, thank goodness, we caught up with you when we did," Jon said.

"I don't like any of what I am hearing," Cam said. "I'm going to have to take very good care of you from now on, Melanie. I won't let you out of my sight."

Melanie smiled. "Well, darling, I do think that is overdoing it. But maybe just for the honeymoon."

Our celebration restored, we cruised around the historic district, down Third Street, tooting the horn, turning onto Nun to pass my house, and through my neighborhood, lowering the windows and waving to neighbors. "We're hitched," Jon called out of the window.

"We are blessed with this weather," Aunt Ruby said. "December 22 and it must be seventy."

"I planned it this way," Melanie said and grinned. She slipped her hand into Cam's. Cameron Jordan, internationally acclaimed television and movie producer, looked as joyful as a little kid on Christmas morning. I've got everything I want now, his expression said.

"This is no where as beautiful as it was on my wedding day," Nelda began, and proceeded to dominate the conversation with a description of her wedding and what she had worn and how she had looked.

We all exchanged looks, wondering when she would end.

But to my surprise, Cam cut her off. "You've got a beautiful soprano singing voice," he said to Scarlett. "Have you ever sung professionally?"

Nelda's jaw fell open. Her son had interrupted her.

Our driver took Dawson to Oleander, heading out through Forest Hills.

"No," she answered, "I've only sung in church."

"Well, I think you sing as good as any professional I've ever heard," Cam said.

"And he would know," Melanie said.

"I've got some contacts. Would you like me to call one of my Broadway producer friends and set up an audition for you?"

Scarlett seemed speechless. "Why . . ." She was momentarily at a loss for words. "Why, yes." She was beaming now. "I'd love that. Do you really think I've got a chance on Broadway? That would be perfect. New York is my home and I miss it. I've been away too long."

Cam leaned forward and spoke earnestly, "I think you've got a very good chance."

"But . . ." Scarlett hesitated. "Maybe I'm too old. I'm past the age of a starlet."

Nelda gave her an appraising look. "How old are you?" she asked sharply.

"Forty," Scarlett said softly.

"Posh, you're a baby. I got some of my best roles when I was forty. Naturally we were not announcing my age, and I looked ten years younger."

"You look very young, Scarlett," Cam agreed. "You don't have to show them your birth certificate. You can pass for thirty any day. I don't think that's a problem. You've got poise. And that voice. And we all know you can dance. Look at Streisand. She's still on top at what? Sixty-five?"

"Thank goodness, the times are changing," Aunt Ruby said. "You know, I think I'll have another glass of champagne."

"Do you really think I've got a chance?" Scarlett asked, her green eyes shining with hope.

Nelda surprised us all by giving her a big smile. "You do

if I say so. Cameron may think he has connections, but he doesn't know who I know." She grinned wickedly. "It's in the bag."

I studied her. Had I just witnessed a miracle?

Binkie lifted the champagne bottle. "Let me refill your glass, Nelda. We're pulling out all the stops tonight. Put my name on your dance card because right after I dance with my bride, I am dancing with you."

21

At Airlie Road, we turned right, passed Airlie Gardens, and then just before we reached the waterway, we pulled into Melanie's private driveway and parked on the circle in front of the hunting lodge. Guests were arriving and filling the spaces around the circle. Two young valets sprang forward, taking keys and moving the cars into the field.

Our little party moved into the lodge to form a receiving line in the vestibule while from the drawing room came the flow of spirited music. The rest of the wedding party, the bridesmaids and groomsmen, surged inside after us. Everyone was talking at once.

Kiki hugged me. "You done good, kid," she said in her Bronx accent. Ray was at her side, but only for a moment, because as soon as he saw Scarlett he was off and running like a bird dog.

"Love is in the air," Kiki said.

"Love? Scarlett?" I asked.

"'Course, Scarlett. What did you think? The woman's a class act. And any sister of yours is a sister of mine." And with that she let out a whoop and a holler and grabbed Melanie in a bear hug and waltzed her around, all the while knowing that Melanie would get flustered and that Melanie was in awe of her and that was a first!

The attendants formed the receiving line with us: the bridesmaids in their pretty red dresses, the groomsmen in tuxedoes.

The guests streamed in and for the next thirty minutes I received hugs, kisses, handshakes, and best wishes. Every so often I'd steal a glance at Jon and he'd look back at me, and we exchanged almost disbelieving looks. We did it! We are married!

Then it was time for the bridal couples to be presented. We paused at the entrance to the drawing room, and the DJ announced: "Ladies and gentlemen, for the first time, may I present Mr. and Mrs. Cameron Jordan and Mr. and Mrs. Jonathan Campbell."

Our guests applauded as a ceremonial piper dressed in a tartan skirt and playing a bagpipe piped the Scottish Campbells and Camerons into the reception.

"The bride and groom's dance," the DJ announced. I moved into Jon's arms as the music played "our" song, Etta James singing "At Last."

The music segued into "What a Wonderful World" with Louis Armstrong singing, and Binkie, Aunt Ruby, Nelda and Granny Campbell joined us on the dance floor. We shared dance partners, cut in on each other, laughed and loved.

Our guests moved out onto the dance floor as the music flowed into "I've Got the World on a String" by Frank Sinatra.

"Look, Jon," I said, indicating Ray and Scarlett. "They are dancing like lovers. Holding each other the way we do."

Jon said, "So it was Scarlett you were seeing. Not Melanie. She was telling the truth all along."

"And I didn't believe her. I feel so guilty."

"Well, don't. Melanie's history would lead anyone to believe what we were thinking. Ray and Scarlett. I like that idea. Logical that he would go for her when she looks so much like Melanie. He is attracted to that type."

"And you? What type are you attracted to?" I asked with a laugh.

"Just wait a few hours. You are going to feel my attraction," Jon said with a grin.

"Promises, promises," I laughed.

Wine and water were being offer to the guests. The DJ said, "Folks, Mrs. Cameron and Mrs. Campbell would like you to join them in the Garden Room. You've all been informed about the little ceremony Mrs. Jordan has planned there, and she's been assured that you are eager to participate in what she calls 'The Kindness Ceremony'."

The guests followed the bridal couples into Melanie's garden room. The room had been filled with flowers. Melanie stood next to the fountain and I stood at her side.

She began the little speech she had prepared. "My sister Ashley and I, and our darling new husbands, want to thank everyone for coming and for sharing this joyous day with us."

"Hear! Hear!" Binkie called.

Melanie smiled. "And now we'll have our little ceremony and we will trust that a lot of good will come out of it," she said sweetly. "First we will have the symbolic drought."

And on cue, one of Elaine's staff cut off the water fountain. Immediately, the water stopped flowing, the sound of the fountain's happy splashing was hushed. Then two waiters with towels came out and mopped out the bowls of the fountain.

"As you know, Ashley and I refused to have a bridal shower and to accept gifts. We have everything we could possibly need. And more. But in many parts of the world, people are in need of the most basic of necessities — water. In some countries, two out of every three people do not have safe, clean drinking water. So if you will file past and fill these bowls with your gifts of money, the funds we collect today will be sent to the Episcopal Relief and Development Ministry so that wells can be dug and water systems installed in Third World countries."

She paused and gave everyone one of her heart-stopping smiles. "I know you will give generously and give us the best wedding present we could ever ask for."

Then we four applauded our guests as the envelopes bulging with money filled the fountain. With laughter and joy, we trooped back to the reception hall for dinner.

While we were gone, the waiters had set out the first course: curried shrimp with melon balls in chilled martini glasses. At every place there were two gift boxes, wrapped in gold paper with red ribbons. Inside were Christmas tree ornaments: white Lennox figurines of a bride and groom, embossed in gold with our names and today's date, December 22, 2007.

Binkie rose from his place at the head table. The music stopped. He tapped his glass with his fork and a hush fell upon the room.

As I gazed up at him, I thought of how he'd always been there for me. How good he was to me. How he had filled the void in my life after my daddy died. I watched with fondness as the familiar lock of snow white hair fell onto his forehead. I wanted to stand up and kiss his forehead but I promised myself I'd do that later.

"Thank you all for sharing this joyous day with us. I know it means a lot to Ashley and Melanie to have you here with us. I've known these girls for many years. And when you are as old as I am," he paused to chuckle, "it is not politically incorrect to call women of their age 'girls'. To me, and to my wife, they have been the daughters we never had. This is the happiest day of their life and, except for the day this lovely lady sitting next to me said yes, it is the happiest of mine."

He lifted his glass. "Ashley, Jon. Melanie, Cameron. I wish you long life and happiness."

"Here. Here." Our guests chanted and toasted us with bubbly.

An endive salad was served next. Not to be outdone, Nelda rose and held her glass aloft dramatically. She still had the ability to command a room and conversation died.

"It is written, when children find true love, parents find true joy," she said. "To my son Cameron and his wife,

Melanie. And to my son's new sister- and brother-in-law, Ashley and Jon. *Salute*!"

For dinner our guests had the choice of a traditional Christmas feast, Beef Wellington with Yorkshire Pudding, or Pasta Primavera. There was roasted green and white asparagus, red and white wine, champagne, and mineral water to go with either.

At one of the round tables, Willie Hudson rose, looking dignified in his tuxedo. His wife of fifty-three years sat at his side. His children and several of his grandchildren who had worked with Jon and me on many restoration projects filled one of the round tables. The little boy who had been our ring bearer sat in his mother's lap.

"Blessed is the day the Lord hath made," Willie said. "And blessed is the day these young people begin life together as newlyweds. My wife, Esther, and I can testify that there is nothing in this world that will buoy you up and keep you strong like a solid, happy marriage. It is the foundation of a good life. That and your church. Those two things and you can withstand just about anything."

He laughed heartily. "Like finding them dead bodies in just about every house I worked on with Jon and Ashley. Me oh my, but that woman sure has a knack for finding them dead bodies! And for getting us involved with murderers."

The room filled with laughter. Willie lifted his glass. "Now Jon, it is up to you. You gotta set this woman on a better course. In all seriousness, I wish Ashley and Jon, and Melanie and Cameron, a life as happy as I've had with my dear wife, Esther."

"Ladies and gentlemen," the DJ said into the microphone. "The father-daughter dance."

Rod Stewart's gravelly voice began to sing, "Have I Told You Lately." I danced with Binkie. Melanie danced with Aunt Ruby. Cam danced with Nelda. Jon danced with Granny Campbell, towering over her by a foot.

Then we all changed partners, and changed partners again. And finally I was in Jon's arms. There were others on the dance floor, but with Jon holding me in his arms, there was no one there but us. The room full of people, the waiters, the DJ, the whole world fell away, as time stood still.

Too quickly we were cutting the cake. Jon's hand covered mine and he said to me so that everyone could hear. "Here's to the prettiest, here's to the wittiest, here's to the truest of all who are true; here's to the neatest one, here's to the sweetest one, here's to them, all in one – here's to you. Ashley, I'll always love you."

On the opposite side of the cake table, Melanie stood with Cam. He had a little speech for her as well. "Happy marriages begin when we marry the one we love, and they blossom when we love the one we married. May our love blossom forever, Melanie dearest."

We fed each cake, a symbol that we would not go hungry in our lives together.

The DJ played one of the songs Jon and I had requested, "Could I Have This Dance" sung by Anne Murray. Jon and I danced and sang the lyrics softly to each.

As the song neared its end, Jon said, "As soon as you toss the bouquet, we are out of here."

I leaned back in his arms to look up at him and asked in mock surprise. "What? Leave our own wedding reception?"

"Ashley, this is Melanie's party. It's not yours. It's not mine. Never has been."

"Yes, my love, you are right about that. But what about Aunt Ruby and Binkie? They'll miss us. And Willie. And what about our clothes? We're in our wedding clothes."

Jon grinned. "There's a change of clothes for us in Melanie's guest room. And your Aunt Ruby packed your suitcases for you. We can make a clean get away."

"So they're in on this too, you scoundrel."

"Yes, they are my co-conspirators. We have our own party to begin, Ashley."

"Are you finally going to share the big secret with me? Are you going to tell me where we're going on our honeymoon?"

"Willie is bringing my car around to the back entrance now. As soon as you toss the bouquet, we'll change and be on our way to Pinehurst."

"Pinehurst. I never would have thought of that. It's so beautiful there."

"Yes, and a short drive. We'll arrive with plenty of energy and in time for bedtime. That is, I'm feeling very energetic. How about you?"

I brushed his lips with mine. "Surprisingly energetic."

"Willie's right. It's up to me to set this woman of mine on a better course. To get you away from Wilmington and these murders you are continually stumbling into. There will be no murders to solve in Pinehurst. Just a few rounds of golf, the

Carolina Inn, biking into the village. Good food. Lots of snuggling. No murder mysteries."

"Yes, darling," I said agreeably, sounding like a good wife. "No more murder mysteries."

But in my heart, I knew better.